## I THOUGHT I KNEW WHAT I WANTED....

Jesse took a small step away from me. "Well, then, good night, Lauren," he said.

"Good night," I said, turning to climb the steps to the house.

"See you around," Jesse called.

"Yeah," I called back as I headed up the stairs, "see ya."

The night had worked out well. Jesse had turned out not to be the jerk I'd expected. In fact, he had turned out to be a pretty nice guy. A really nice guy, actually. A guy I could talk to.

But I still didn't want a boyfriend. And he didn't want a girlfriend.

*Yes,* I thought, *tonight had been a good thing.* Better than I could have hoped for.

*Why, then,* I wondered as I flicked on the bathroom light, *do I feel my heart sinking?*

Don't miss any of the books in *Love Stories*
—the romantic series from Bantam Books!

*Love Stories*

# Up ALL Night

## Karen Michaels

BANTAM BOOKS
NEW YORK · TORONTO · LONDON · SYDNEY · AUCKLAND

*To Rose and Arthur, the best aunt and uncle
in the world, and always to Mike.*

RL 6, age 12 and up

UP ALL NIGHT

*A Bantam Book / March 1997*

*Produced by Daniel Weiss Associates, Inc.
33 West 17th Street
New York, NY 10011.
Cover photography by Michael Segal.*

ISBN: 0-553-57047-1

*Published simultaneously in the United States and Canada*

*Bantam Books are published by Bantam Books, a division of Bantam
Doubleday Dell Publishing Group, Inc. Its trademark, consisting of the
words "Bantam Books" and the portrayal of a rooster, is Registered in
U.S. Patent and Trademark Office and in other countries. Marca
Registrada. Bantam Books, 1540 Broadway, New York, New York 10036.*

PRINTED IN THE UNITED STATES OF AMERICA

OPM     0 9 8 7 6 5 4 3 2 1

# PROLOGUE

I MAY BE only fifteen years old, but as of this month, I have made two vows for life. Number one: I will never be stupid enough to believe in love. Number two: I will never play bridge.

Most people don't have the foresight to make these vows. Take my parents, for instance. If they had sworn off love and bridge a long time ago, I wouldn't be gearing up right now for the worst summer of my life—maybe even the worst summer in the history of summer. But then again, my parents aren't exactly the most considerate people on the planet.

Perhaps I should explain.

About eight months ago my father moved out of our house and into the new town house development near his office. At first I was miserable, but my parents kept telling me that it was only a "trial separation." They said it didn't mean anything that drastic, that they just had some things to work out and it would be easier to do that under separate roofs.

Now you might be saying, "Hello, Lauren, wake up and smell the coffee. What kind of marriage problems are actually *solved* by living apart?" But I really believed them when they said it was only temporary. Besides, since he was living so close, I still saw my father almost every day. The three of us had dinner together once a week, which, thanks to my parents' busy schedules, was pretty much the same as when we'd all lived together.

I guess I'd been pretty stupid to think things would just go back to normal, but I did. So, despite my parents' separation, I had actually been having a pretty good year. School was probably as good as school could be. I was the first sophomore to be the photography editor of the school newspaper. I had just won first prize in Walt Whitman High School's spring photography competition. Last, and certainly not least, I was finally going to get my braces off.

It seemed like I'd been a metal mouth for much longer than two years. I couldn't wait to be liberated. But it wasn't the goofiness of my appearance that made me so conscious of the braces and so eager to be rid of them. Let's just say that when your dad is your orthodontist, braces tend to come up in conversation more often than not.

Most people are off the hook. Most people visit their orthodontist every six weeks or so. You can forget to put in the rubber bands, not wear your headgear . . . pretty much slack off in general and no one would be the wiser. Not so for me. My checkups were nearly nightly. And as much as I hated it, I couldn't exactly blame my father for being overly concerned. Teeth were his life. Besides, what kind of orthodontist lets his only child's teeth stay crooked?

Finally, a little more than two months ago, the big day had arrived. I'd sat in the chair as my father removed the metal from my mouth. I felt like a prisoner being released from handcuffs. Since my braces had been such a big part of life in our family, it seemed natural that getting them off would be a special occasion. My mother had left work early to meet us at my dad's office so we could all go out for a festive dinner at Callahan's, my favorite restaurant. She arrived just as Dad was finishing up.

"Lauren, your father and I have something to tell you," she said after about a minute.

I was still lying in the chair, wearing the bib and everything, totally unprepared for what happened next.

They told me they were getting a divorce.

I can't remember who said it or how, but it went something like, "We're pulling the rug out from under you; now rinse."

Then we went to Callahan's. The whole time my parents kept telling me how their divorce had nothing to do with their feelings for me and that they both wanted what was best for the family. I had to keep licking my freshly bared teeth to remind myself that I was supposed to feel festive. I'd been dreaming about Callahan's spinach and artichoke dip for the past two years—and even though it would no longer get caught between the wires in my mouth, I had suddenly lost the desire to pig out.

"Things are going to be different," my mother said. "But one thing will never, ever change. We will always love you."

"I know," I mumbled. I was seriously on the verge of losing my cool and blubbering right there at the table, but I still blurted out a question. "But what about working things out? You always said the separation was only temporary." Hearing the quiver in my voice, I bit extra hard into a dip-heavy tortilla chip.

"We didn't know for sure what was going to happen," my father said, laying a hand on my shoulder. "And we didn't want you to think the worst until we decided. The important thing now is that you know that no matter what happens, you will always come first with us."

"Right," my mother had agreed. "Just because we're ending our marriage doesn't mean we're going to be at each other's throats."

All I could do was nod.

Well, that sentiment lasted for about two days. Then the gloves came off. The past two months have been like World War III, with my parents arguing over everything from health insurance to the carousel horse we have in the den.

The divorce really shouldn't have been all that surprising, and maybe if I hadn't believed my parents when they said they were trying to work things out, it wouldn't have been. I asked my father for a concrete explanation.

"Maybe you can't understand this now, but we've really been drifting apart for years," he said. "And once we were living apart, we saw that we had just grown too far away from each other to stay husband and wife."

That didn't do it for me, so I asked my mother.

"I don't know how it happened," she said. "We just don't feel the same way about each other as we did when we were first married. It's sad, but your father and I don't have much besides you in common anymore."

I'd never really thought about my parents as being in love or whatever—they were just my parents, you know? But looking back on things now, I can kind of see what they meant. Even before Dad moved out, they had always had semiseparate interests. My mother spent her free time with friends from work and my dad spent his in our driveway, restoring old cars. I still had a great relationship with both of them, but I can't remember the three of us doing many things together as a family other than the vacations we took to Martha's Vineyard when I was a kid—or the two of them doing anything together as a couple except for playing bridge. And both of those activities involved the Hillmans.

My parents are big bridge players. They take the

game very seriously. In fact, the only times I ever remembered my parents yelling at each other *before* the divorce announcement was when one of them had played badly. Ever since I was little, they would get together with Mr. and Mrs. Hillman every other Thursday and break out the cards. I guess the Hillmans were probably my parents' best friends, if parents even work that way.

That's the way it used to be, but now everything has changed. First of all, my parents don't play bridge with the Hillmans anymore. Marilyn Hillman calls my mother every day, even though she is "staying impartial." Since the Hillmans are such good friends, they have invited me to spend the summer on the Vineyard with them so that I can get away from my parents' fighting.

Under different circumstances, this plan would be terrific. I've always loved Martha's Vineyard. In fact, the picture I won the photography prize for was taken on a dock there at sunrise two years ago. What would make it even better is that the Hillmans have a great house on the Vineyard, perfectly situated on the beach and in walking distance from town. When I was really young, I would spend the whole summer there with the Hillmans, and my parents would come on the weekends and for the last three weeks. When I was older, we would rent a house in Chilmark for three weeks in August. Sometimes, instead of bothering to rent our own house for our annual August three-week vacation, my parents and I would just stay with the Hillmans.

But we hadn't done that in years. In fact, over the past three years our Vineyard vacation time had dropped from three weeks to ten days. Last year my mom and I went for a week alone and stayed at one of those cute Victorian inns in Oak Bluffs. My dad had come for the weekend but had spent most of his time playing in the tennis tournament at the Beach Club.

In a way, I am really excited to be spending a full summer there. Martha's Vineyard is truly like another world. Biking around the island, with its old houses and narrow roads and the ocean breeze in your hair, you really do feel a million miles away from regular life, which is just what I need right about now. And the Hillmans are practically my second parents.

The only problem is that their daughter will be there too.

Rachel Hillman used to be my best friend, with emphasis on *used to*. We shared everything when we were in elementary school and even in junior high—toys, clothes, hobbies. But by the beginning of this year, it was obvious to both of us that we'd gone in two completely different directions.

Let's face it, photography and the newspaper don't exactly mix with the Pommies—the cheerleading squad that comes out during halftime at football games to do goofy routines to cheesy songs. At the end of freshman year Rachel decided to try out. We were still friends then, but not as close as we'd been, and I'd had no idea that she was going to do it. We were walking down the hall after lunch one day when I'd noticed a sign for the Pommie tryouts.

"Who would do that?" I'd asked rhetorically. "Cheerleading is so lame."

"I'm trying out," Rachel had replied. The stony look on her face told me she wasn't joking. I knew I had just put my foot in my mouth big time.

"Rachel, I had no idea you were into that," I'd said, attempting some damage control. "I was only kidding. I mean, the Pommies are more like dancers than cheerleaders."

"Yeah, right. Just because I don't like hanging out with those brainy geeks from the paper like you do doesn't mean I can't have my own interests."

"Nobody said you couldn't." I tried to ignore the implications of her "brainy geek" statement. "I'm just surprised that you'd go out for the Pommies."

"Well, maybe there's a lot about me that you don't understand," Rachel had stated.

"Apparently," I'd agreed. Luckily the bell rang, and it was safe to mumble our good-byes and walk off in separate directions.

That had probably been the longest conversation we'd had in the past year. First we stopped calling each other every night. We would say "hi" to each other in the hall, but over time it became obvious that we had nothing else to say.

After what happened last winter, even "hi's" have stopped.

One night over dinner my father had asked me why I never talked about Rachel anymore.

"I don't know." I'd shrugged, twirling linguine around my fork. "We don't really hang out that much these days."

"Why's that?" he'd asked as he ripped a piece of garlic bread off the loaf.

"We don't have much in common," I answered simply.

"Since when?" Dad's eyebrow was raised inquisitively. He was taking a real interest in this.

How do you explain these kinds of things to parents? "It's just that we have different friends now," I offered. "We're not exactly in the same circle."

It was true. I hung out with Becky Young and the rest of the newspaper staff. When she wasn't practicing with the Pommies, Rachel could be found giggling and flirting with Eric Arlen and the rest of the school jocks.

"Well, maybe you two should spend some time together alone, without those other friends," Dad recommended.

"Yeah, maybe," I replied.

Later that night, as I was spacing out over my math homework, I thought about my father's suggestion. Even though I had plenty of friends, I had sort of missed Rachel. Why not try to do something together like old times?

After second period the next day I approached Rachel's locker with a sense of purpose. As I got closer I could see her leaning against her locker, batting her eyes at Eric Arlen.

*So what?* I thought as I continued down the hall. *Just because I think Eric Arlen is a dumb jock doesn't mean that Rachel can't like him if she wants.*

"Hey, Rach," I said when I reached her.

Rachel turned at the sound of her name. When she saw me standing behind her, she said a quick "Hi" and whipped back around to face Eric again.

"I was thinking," I continued, determined to repair our once strong friendship, "maybe we could do something together this weekend. Maybe take the T and go to Faneuil Hall like old times."

When she turned around again, the look on Rachel's face was clearly one of surprise. I just couldn't tell if it was pleasant surprise.

"I know it's kind of out of left field . . . ," I said hesitatingly.

"Yeah," she replied. "And it's nice of you to ask. But I'm, um, kind of busy this weekend. . . ." Rachel's voice trailed off as she glanced back at Eric, who was looking back and forth at the two of us as if this was the strangest conversation in history.

"Well," I responded, nodding understandingly, "maybe some other time."

"Sure, Lauren," Rachel said, turning away with what I sensed was relief.

Clutching my books to my chest, I spun on my heels. Had I just acted like a total loser? Where

Rachel's and my relationship stood, in that weird no-man's-land between friend and enemy, I couldn't be sure. *Whatever,* I told myself. *She was busy.*

I had almost convinced myself of that when I heard Eric Arlen's booming jock voice.

"*You're* friends with *her?*" he asked with apparent shock.

"Well, kind of," Rachel answered quickly. "It's more like our parents are friends, so—"

"Oh," Eric answered. "It's one of *those* things."

I felt the heat of anger rush up the back of my neck. So that's how Rachel felt. I was one of those "I don't really like you, but I have to hang out with you anyway" people to her now—like some annoying younger cousin. Here I'd done the nice thing, trying to restore our friendship, and she made me out to be some dweeb to impress Eric Arlen.

Feeling like I should say something, I'd whipped back around to see Rachel and Eric deep in flirt mode. She looked like some cheerleader in an after-school special with her long blond hair, big blue eyes, and perfect teeth. *This* was the person I was trying so hard to be friends with? Why was I even wasting my time? Maybe it was better this way; at least I knew what Rachel thought of me.

I'd turned and headed off to third period, determined never to take my father's advice again.

So while it's not as if Rachel and I are mortal enemies or anything, we're about as far from being friends as two people can get. And we are definitely *not* a pair who should be spending the entire summer together.

Unfortunately my mother was totally oblivious to the situation with Rachel and me. Before I could even protest, she went ahead and cemented the plans with Mrs. Hillman. Now there was no way that I *couldn't* go to Martha's Vineyard. I tried to explain to her just how disastrous this would be.

"I don't understand," she said. "Are you and Rachel in some kind of fight?"

"No, it's not that," I replied.

"Well, then, I don't see the problem."

"It's complicated," I argued. "We don't speak each other's language anymore."

"That's silly. You two have been friends since you were in diapers." She hugged me. "Even if you haven't been as close lately, this summer will be a great chance for you to spend some time together. You can patch things up before you lose a very special friendship."

I untangled myself from her embrace, in no mood to be comforted. "I don't see what's so special about a friend who you have nothing in common with," I said.

"Well, would you rather stay here?"

I couldn't really answer. My mom had a point. Almost anything was preferable to spending the summer in this war zone.

"Honey," she went on, "I'm sure you'll work it

out. When you and Rachel were little, you used to fight all the time. It would last about an hour, and then you'd make up. I give you two weeks until you're back to normal."

"I doubt it," I muttered. And I thought: *If it's so easy to patch things up, why don't you try that with Dad?*

# ONE

"LAUREN?" MY MOTHER called from the kitchen. "Are you ready, honey?"

I grunted in response.

"Lauren?" she called again.

"I'll be right there!" I yelled, glaring at the closed bedroom door.

I shook my head. I couldn't believe the day of my departure for Martha's Vineyard had finally arrived. The morning sun was shining with deceptive cheerfulness. Every last minute attempt to find some other solution—getting a job, enrolling in summer school, entering into an exchange program that would send me to Switzerland—had failed. I was going to spend the summer with Rachel Hillman. There was nothing I could do about it.

I zipped up my soft-pack duffel bag and took one last long look at the forlorn face in the mirror above my bureau.

My parents always used to joke that I looked like Little Orphan Annie because of my freckles and long, curly red hair—and because I'm so skinny. Well, at that moment I actually *felt* like her. How was I any different? I was being sent away from my own home to stay with a family that only wanted me because they felt sorry for me.

I slung the bag over my shoulder and headed out the door. I was about halfway down the stairs when I heard my parents' voices in the kitchen.

"I canceled all my morning patients, Carol," my father was saying. "How can you say you didn't know I was taking her?"

"Very easily, because I had no idea," replied my mother. "Your communication skills are lacking as usual, Alan."

True to form, they were arguing. I sighed. It was another banner day in the Tyler house.

"Well, I'm here now, so I'll drive Lauren," my father insisted.

"You can't just walk in here and lay down the law," my mother said, slamming a cabinet door. "You always think you can make all the decisions, no discussion necessary! Well, it doesn't work that way. *I'm* taking Lauren to the Vineyard. We have a ten-thirty ferry reservation. I told Marilyn we'd be there before lunch."

"I've rearranged my schedule, Carol!" my dad shouted. "I know you're doing this just to spite me!"

"To spite you! Lauren's my daughter too!"

I couldn't take it anymore. I stormed into the

kitchen. "When you're done fighting, I'll be in the car," I snapped. Before they could reply, I marched out to the Jeep and slammed the door.

After about a minute my father climbed into the driver's seat. He opened his mouth as if he were about to say something, then shut it and started the engine. I decided not to talk to him. Instead I stared out the window in silence as we headed out of our driveway and onto the road.

My mother came out the front door and waved good-bye. Her face was creased with guilt and worry, but she forced a strained smile. "Have a good time!" she shouted as we pulled away.

I just nodded. *Good-bye, house,* I said silently. *Good-bye, tree. Good-bye, mailbox.*

"Lauren, I'm sorry about that." My father took a deep breath. "And I'm sure your mother is too. We didn't mean to upset you. It was just a stupid misunderstanding."

"You two could set a world record for misunderstandings," I muttered.

"You're right." He sighed. "I wish it could be different, but right now I don't see how."

I folded my arms over my chest. What was there to say?

After a few minutes he spoke again. "Well, I'm sure you're glad to be rid of us," he said with a half-hearted grin, trying to be funny. "And you're finally getting to spend another whole summer out on the Vineyard. You were always saying that your mother and I should stay out there for a *real* vacation."

I didn't answer out loud. I was too busy thinking about all of the other ways he and Mom had failed me. Not spending a full summer on the Vineyard was just the tip of the iceberg.

"And it'll give you and Rachel a chance to spend some time together." Dad's voice was filled with that look-on-the-bright-side cheery optimism that can really get on my nerves.

"Yup," I answered without emotion. I'd never told my father what had happened when I'd followed his advice and asked Rachel to hang out. I knew it would only lead to some pep talk about friends being the most important thing we have and not letting them go. I definitely wasn't in the mood for that speech now.

"This summer is going to do you a world of good, Lauren," he added. "You won't have to live with the fighting, and by the time you get back, I'm sure things will be resolved. Then we can all make a fresh start."

"Great," I said unenthusiastically.

"I know you don't believe this now, but once everything is settled, things are going to be great. Your mom and I will be happier. You'll be happier. It will be a whole new chapter in our lives. Everything's going to be better. You'll see."

I just shook my head. "No offense, Dad, but I'm getting really sick of you and Mom telling me how everything's going to be fine and dandy. Especially since it always ends up being exactly the opposite."

He bit his lip. "Lauren, divorce is hard on

everyone," he said softly. "You know that your mother and I would never do anything to hurt you deliberately."

"I know, I know," I grumbled. "I've just had enough of hearing the same old crap."

He tried to smile again. "Well, then, I bet you can't wait to get to the beach."

"Whatever."

We rode the rest of the way to Woods Hole without speaking, and as soon as we boarded the ferry I bolted out of the car to the upper deck. Riding the ferry from Woods Hole to Vineyard Haven has always been one of the special things about Martha's Vineyard. The last thing I wanted was another "everything's going to work out, you're so important to us" speech from my dad. It would only ruin the mood.

Leaning over the ferry rail, I breathed in the Martha's Vineyard ocean air. It was that same salty-clean smell that I always anticipated. That familiar smell of freedom, of that carefree time when the school year really feels over and the next one seems too far away to be real. With the summer wind in my hair, I almost forgot the mess that my life had become.

I almost forgot, but not quite.

# TWO

"DON'T FEEL LIKE you have to hang out with us, Lauren," Mrs. Hillman said as she re-filled her glass with iced tea. "You can head upstairs and get settled in."

I nodded. Mr. and Mrs. Hillman, my dad, and I had been sitting on the Hillmans' patio, drinking iced tea and making small talk for the past twenty minutes. I knew that the offer was code for "we don't want to discuss the gory details of your parents' divorce right in front of your face."

"Yeah, I guess I'll go up to the guest room and unpack," I said.

"The guest room?" Mr. Hillman asked, his eyebrow arching.

"I just thought . . ." I let the sentence hang. In all the years I'd come to Martha's Vineyard with the Hillmans, I had never actually stayed in the guest room; my parents had. I had always shared the killer third–floor suite with Rachel. But this time I felt funny about it. Knowing the situation between Rachel and me, I figured that I'd be staying in the guest room. Rachel probably wanted it that way.

"You're staying on the third floor with Rachel," Mrs. Hillman said, looking puzzled. "She cleared off the other bed and everything."

I wondered how the Hillmans had twisted Rachel's arm to get her to agree to *that* setup. But maybe it wouldn't be so bad. I actually felt a trace of nostalgia. After all, some of the best times I had spent on the Vineyard had been in that room. It wouldn't feel like summer if I stayed somewhere else.

"Then I guess I'll head up there," I said, grabbing my duffel bag.

"Rachel should be back any minute to help you unpack," Mr. Hillman said, looking at his watch. "We told her you'd be here at noon."

"Great," I said, flashing a fake smile.

"Honey, I might as well say good-bye to you now," my father said as he came over to hug me. He sighed. "We'll miss you, but we know that you'll have a great time here."

I pulled away from him. "I know, Dad," I said quickly, walking away so that I wouldn't cry. The way he kept saying "we" was weird, like he and Mom were still a "we."

"Why don't you change into beach clothes while you're at it?" Mrs. Hillman called after me.

I had decided to travel light, so it only took

about ten minutes to put my clothes away and stick my toiletries bag in the bathroom. As I buckled up the overalls I'd put on over my blue one-piece bathing suit, I wondered if it was too soon to head back down to the patio.

"You all settled in?"

I almost jumped. I hadn't heard Rachel enter— but there she was, standing before me, looking as if she'd just come in from a serious tanning session. Her hair was so blond that it looked bleached. I hoped she hadn't put peroxide in it.

"Yeah," I said. "Thanks for leaving me the top drawers."

She smiled. "Of course. You always get the top two so I can have the extra one on the bottom. Remember?"

"Yeah . . . I guess some things never change," I said.

"Guess not," she replied a little awkwardly.

For a minute neither one of us said anything. I rolled up the cuffs of my overalls and put on some sandals.

"Is that what you're wearing?" Rachel asked, glancing over my outfit.

"Yeah," I replied, unsure why she was asking.

Rachel raised her eyebrows. "You know that we're going to the Beach Club for lunch."

"Yeah, so?" I was confused. The Beach Club had a formal dining room inside, but it was only used for dinners and big events like the annual Midsummer Ball. I had assumed that we were having lunch at the outdoor restaurant, the Ocean Café. There was no dress code there. Most people came straight from the beach, in just their bathing suits. Mrs. Hillman had said to wear "beach clothes." In fact, Rachel herself was only wearing a red bikini.

"So . . . what I mean is, it's the beginning of the summer," Rachel said. "It's important to make a good first impression."

I frowned. "What first impression? For who?" I was starting to get a little annoyed by the tone of her voice. Besides, I wasn't here to impress anybody.

She let out a slight chuckle. "All I'm saying, Lauren, is that no guy is going to notice you if you dress like Farmer Joe."

I couldn't help but smirk. I should have known. Now that Pommie season was over, Rachel obviously had a one-track mind. No wonder her bathing suit was so skimpy. All the better for her to attract attention.

"For your information, Rachel," I said, "I could care less if any guy notices me."

She shrugged. "Whatever you say," she answered in a singsong voice.

I started to get angry. I couldn't help myself. "Believe it or not, some of us have better things to do than worry about guys twenty-four hours a day."

"That's right," Rachel said sarcastically. "I forgot. People on the newspaper are above us mere teenagers."

I sighed. "Listen, Rachel. I never said I was above you. All I said is that I don't feel the need to parade around in some tiny bathing suit just to impress some stupid guy. It's not something I care about."

"Oh, you care plenty," Rachel responded. She tossed her hair over her shoulders and left the room. "You're just scared to death of it actually *happening*. Face it, Lauren: You're scared of guys."

I opened my mouth, but for some reason no words would come. I listened to her footsteps as they faded down the stairs. All I could do was stand there, staring through the empty doorway like an idiot. I'd been with Rachel for less than three minutes, and we had already gotten into a fight. Would this summer be even more of a catastrophe than I'd anticipated?

"Lauren, are you coming?" Mrs. Hillman called from downstairs.

"I—I just have to put on some sunblock!" I yelled back. "I'll meet you there."

There was a pause. "Okay. See you in a bit." The front door slammed.

I flopped down on the bed, utterly miserable. I could see it now: I was going to spend the rest of the summer making excuses to avoid Rachel. The situation was hopeless. Still, it was *her* fault. Where did she come off saying I was afraid of guys? After all, she knew that *I* was the one who had been kissed first. Even if it was in sixth grade and during

23

one of those "four minutes in the closet" games, I had kissed a guy before Rachel ever had.

And it wasn't like I'd never had a boyfriend either. All first semester I'd been sort of seeing Jonathan Groff. He was the editor of the school newspaper, so there was no way that Rachel wouldn't have noticed—especially since Jonathan and I showed up together at the homecoming dance. Of course, he'd ended up leaving with Cori Schreiber, but I hadn't really cared. I mean, it wasn't like he was *really* my boyfriend. To me, Jonathan had been more someone to have as a date than someone to actually care about.

Besides, under the present circumstances it was only natural that I wouldn't be bending over backward to find a guy. My parents' divorce wasn't exactly an inspiration in the romance department.

I resolved to prove to Rachel that she was wrong. My lack of interest in flirting with every male on the planet had nothing to do with fear. Nothing at all.

I smeared myself in sunblock and headed to the back porch and down the little stairway that went straight to the beach. For a moment I just stood next to the bottom step, listening to the breaking waves and basking in the early afternoon sun. Finally I sighed and hopped on my bike, which my dad had taken out of the trunk and left on the Hillmans' patio. Pedaling out onto the main road, I began making my way toward the Beach Club—a sprawling wooden building with a huge deck and tennis courts on one side. It was barely a hundred yards away. The island breeze blew in my hair as I rode the familiar old route.

*This is going to be a long couple of months.*

It seemed as if I had repeated those words to myself a thousand times already. If it wasn't for my parents, I wouldn't have even *been* here. I squinted, trying to spot Mr. and Mrs. Hillman on the deck, where we would be eating lunch. Why was it that *they* could get along and my parents couldn't? What secret did they have?

I knew there had been a time when my parents had been totally in love with each other. I had the videotape to prove it—the video from my parents' wedding. My mother had looked so beautiful in the antique white lace wedding dress that she'd borrowed from her mother. It had a full skirt that spun out as my father twirled her around the dance floor.

"Alan!" she had screamed, shrieking with laughter. "Alan! You're making me dizzy!"

"I can't help it." He had spun her faster. "I'm crazy with love!"

Then he'd stopped, and they'd kissed. My mother had turned to the camera and said, "Steve, get that camera off of us; this is going to get X-rated!" My father put his hand over the lens, but you could still hear them laughing.

My uncle Steve must have turned the camera off because the next thing on the tape was Grandpa Bert making a long, boring toast.

I used to love watching their wedding video—mostly because my parents looked so corny. I hoped they wouldn't get rid of the tape. They'd paid a lot to get it converted from the original film to a videotape. When I got home from this trip, I would watch it over and over to remind myself that love, marriage, and the rest of it was a total sham.

The Hillmans were still nowhere to be seen, so I locked my bike on the rack and headed through the gates and up the ramp toward the other side of the deck. For the first time ever I felt strange and out of place at the Beach Club. Even more than Rachel's bedroom, it seemed to represent a past that had disappeared forever. The Beach Club had been a part of every summer I'd spent here. Rachel and I had even gone to the club's day camp when we were little.

Back then we had fantasized about working at the club together when we were older. We had planned to live together in the staff bungalows, which mostly consisted of high-school and college kids who, like me, normally lived in the suburbs of Boston or Connecticut. Rachel and I had always thought that working at the Beach Club would be the coolest way to spend a summer.

Well, at least our spat had made one thing clear—we weren't going to be sharing any more fantasies about the future.

As I made my way across the deck to the café I spotted Rachel—red bikini, sunglasses, and all—sitting alone at a table. A guy who bore an amazing resemblance to a Ken doll hovered around her, adjusting the table's umbrella. His pink polo shirt and white Bermuda shorts indicated that he was a waiter at the club. I couldn't help but roll my eyes. Rachel wasted *no* time.

For a second I seriously considered bolting and trying to find Rachel's parents. I really didn't feel like sitting at the table while Rachel tried to break a Guinness record for most obvious flirt. But it was too late—she had already spotted me. She flashed me a big fake smile and waved me over. I took a deep breath, forcing my feet to move in her direction.

"Did you get your sunblock on?" Rachel asked as I approached. I could tell she'd seen my excuse for not walking over with her for exactly what it was—an excuse.

"I think I managed," I said, matching her phoniness.

"I'm Kyle Shaw," the Ken doll said. He smiled and held out his hand.

I shook his hand blandly. "Hi."

"Kyle, meet Lauren Tyler," Rachel said. "She's staying with us for the summer."

"Great," he said. The broad, toothy smile on his face showed no signs of drooping anytime soon.

"Yeah." I nodded, silently adding, *Not really*.

"Are you two related?" Kyle asked.

"No." I pulled out the chair across from Rachel's and slumped into it. Even if she and I were pretending to be buddies, I wasn't about to sit down next to her.

"Our parents are best friends," Rachel explained, grinning up at Kyle. "This place was our main food source when we were kids."

"Oh," he said, turning his gaze back to me. "Are your parents members also?"

"No," I said. We used to be the Hillmans' guests at the club, but I didn't feel like explaining that to Kyle the Smile. I'd had enough of thinking and talking about the past.

"Speaking of your parents," I said to Rachel, "aren't they supposed to be here?"

"They're reserving a tennis court for later," Rachel explained.

"Oh." I hoped that wouldn't take too long. As much as Rachel's new friend annoyed me, I knew he'd probably have to get back to work soon—leaving Rachel and me alone there together. I would have to be sure to go to the bathroom when that happened.

"Hey, wait a minute," Kyle said excitedly. "This is perfect."

I raised my eyebrows. "What is?"

"You staying with Rachel!"

"Why's that?" I asked, very much doubting that anything Kyle had in mind would be "perfect."

"Because I'm working here at the club this summer along with my cousin. Now the two of you can join Rachel and me tonight."

*Of course,* I thought. I should have known to expect a lame suggestion. But before I could even refuse, Rachel spoke up.

"That's sweet of you, Kyle," she said. "But I doubt Lauren is interested."

"Come on," Kyle urged me. "We'll make a great foursome."

Once again Rachel decided to answer for me. "I don't think a double *date* is really Lauren's thing," she explained, sneaking a look at me.

So that was it. Rachel was taking this opportunity to prove that I *was* afraid of guys. And even though I was absolutely positive that Kyle, Kyle's cousin, Rachel, and I would *not* make "a great foursome," there was no way I could refuse without making Rachel feel as if she'd won our argument.

*So what?* I thought. *Let her believe what she wants. It doesn't matter.*

Rachel stared at me from across the table. Her expression seemed to scream "I told you so."

Without another moment's hesitation I turned to Kyle. "Why not?" I said as cheerfully as I could.

"So you'll come?" Kyle said, his perma-grin widening.

"What the heck," I said. I glanced at Rachel. The smug look had disappeared from her face. "I'm psyched to meet some new people," I added, just for dramatic effect.

"Great!" Kyle said. "So we'll meet you both back here at eight?"

"Sounds good," I replied.

"I'll see you guys later, then." He turned to

Rachel apologetically. "I should get back to work now."

Rachel flashed him a smile. "See you at eight."

As soon as Kyle waved good-bye and walked away, Rachel's smile vanished.

"Okay, Lauren," she said. Her tone was completely different than the phony-friendly one she'd been using in Kyle's presence. "You've proved your point."

"Why . . . what are you talking about, Rachel?" I asked, playing dumb. "You don't think I'll *chicken out* or something, do you? After all, I *am* afraid of guys."

Rachel sighed. "Okay, Lauren," she said, fidgeting with her silverware. "You win. I take back what I said. You're not afraid of guys."

"Good," I replied. "I don't know why you said it in the first place."

"I'm sure you don't," Rachel mumbled, looking away from me and out toward the ocean.

"What is that supposed to mean?"

The corners of Rachel's mouth twisted sourly. "I heard you talking to Becky Young in the cafeteria. You couldn't stop ragging on me for hanging out with Eric Arlen. You said something like, 'She must have at least a million cavities from all that disgusting sweetness.'"

I felt myself flush. Although I couldn't remember the exact conversation, it did sound like something I would have said. But why should I feel bad about it? "Well, that was only after I heard you tell

Eric that I was just a friend of the family, not an actual friend of *yours*," I said, trying to sound less defensive than I felt.

Now it was Rachel's turn to redden. It was obvious from the way she avoided my eyes that she knew exactly what I meant. We sure were getting things right out in the open.

"I don't know why I said that to Eric," Rachel said, twisting a piece of napkin. "I just didn't know how to explain what we were. It was the easiest thing to tell him."

Something in Rachel's tone made me soften. Maybe she hadn't meant to be so harsh. Besides, hearing me talk to Becky about her must have struck Rachel as pretty brutal as well. I was willing to call a truce.

"Well, things between the two of us have been kind of weird lately," I said.

"Yeah." She nodded. "I know."

Neither of us said anything for a moment. I tried to focus on the buzz of conversations at neighboring tables.

"Well, it looks like we have plans tonight," Rachel said finally. "Who knows? Maybe Kyle's cousin will turn out to be the man of your dreams."

I snorted in response.

Rachel shrugged. "You know what they say . . . 'When you least expect it, expect it.'"

"Let's get one thing straight, Rachel," I said matter-of-factly. "I may have agreed to go out with you tonight—but there's absolutely no way that this is going to be some kind of a date."

"Oh, I don't know about that," Rachel said teasingly. "Two guys, two girls, romantic walks down the beach in the moonlight. Sounds like date material to me."

"Fine," I said, exasperated. "Have it your way. It's a date. Satisfied?"

Rachel simply shrugged. "I guess you didn't really prove me wrong at all. You're still afraid of guys."

I knew she was just kidding, but it bugged me anyway. "For your information," I explained calmly, "I am *not* afraid of guys. But unlike *you,* I didn't come here to meet some dork and have a stupid summer fling. That kind of stuff only happens in bad movies."

Rachel just looked at me for a moment. "You can have whatever bitter attitude you want, Lauren," she said quietly. "Just don't ruin my date, okay?"

"I could care less about your date," I snapped. "All I want is for you to get off my back."

Rachel didn't say anything. For a moment I felt bad. It wasn't as if I wanted to spoil Rachel's fun or anything. Even if her idea of fun *was* totally lame. I cleared my throat to apologize, but before I could say anything, Rachel spoke up.

"Let's make a deal," she offered. "I'll promise to leave you alone about dating if you'll promise to at least be civil to Kyle's cousin."

I thought about that for a second. Even though I

still felt guilty, I couldn't help but realize that Rachel was so concerned with her love life that I now had some power over her. And it was power that I intended to use. "You'll leave me alone for the rest of the summer?" I asked, making sure of the terms.

She nodded. "But only if you don't do anything to make tonight unbearable. Or do anything to embarrass me in front of Kyle."

"Nothing more about me and any guy, real or imaginary?" I asked.

Rachel rolled her eyes.

"Then it's a deal," I said, feeling a sense of victory.

She sighed. "Good."

Suddenly Mr. Hillman's voice boomed across the deck. "There you are! I hope you two didn't order without us."

As I turned in his direction I caught a glimpse of Kyle. He stood a couple of tables away, leaning over a very pretty brunette. It was a position almost identical to the one I'd seen him in with Rachel just a few minutes before. The girl was giggling flirtatiously, just as Rachel had.

I looked over to Rachel to see if she had noticed, but she was looking down at her menu.

*That guy is one smooth operator,* I thought. My dislike for Kyle Shaw was growing.

"Sorry it took us so long, girls. But hey, look who we ran into," Mrs. Hillman said, smiling as she approached.

I forced myself to smile back as Mr. and Mrs. Hillman sat down at the table with us, followed by Tommy Davis.

I actually really liked Tommy. Rachel and I had been friends with him since we were little because all three of us spent our summers on the Vineyard. He was from a neighboring suburb of Boston, but I hardly saw him during the school year. He looked pretty much the same to me— dirty blond hair, green eyes. I noticed that he did look a lot taller.

"Hey," Tommy said, coming over to give each of us a hug, "it's good to see you guys."

"It's good to see you too," I told him.

"Yeah," Rachel said. "Do you want to sit down with us?"

Tommy looked at his watch. "Sure, for a little while." He pulled out a chair. "My shift starts in twenty minutes."

"Where are you working this summer?" Mr. Hillman asked Tommy.

"I'm lifeguarding at the pool," he answered, leaning back in his chair.

"That's great." Rachel smiled. "You always said that you wanted to be a lifeguard."

"Yup. And I finally got my certification." Tommy paused and looked at Rachel and me for a moment. "So how's the dynamic duo doing?" he asked, referring to the two of us.

There was an awkward pause for a moment. *Wow, he really hasn't seen us in a while,* I thought.

"We're doing fine," Rachel said quickly. "How's everything with you?"

Well, *he* certainly didn't seem to notice the tension between Rachel and me. Or if he did, he was doing a great job of ignoring it. Still, I was beginning to feel a little better. At least things were settled.

All I had to do now was endure that stupid date.

# THREE

"I DON'T KNOW," Rachel was saying as she stared at herself in the mirror. "I think it looks too obvious."

I looked up from Rachel's issue of *Seventeen*. "Obvious in what way?"

Rachel turned away from the mirror long enough to give me a look that said: "Duh." Then she returned to smoothing out the bottom of her short black dress. It was the third outfit she'd tried on in the past twenty minutes. I assumed it was about to be rejected just like the ones before. Each of them looked fine to me, but apparently Rachel had a more developed sense of fashion than I did.

"It makes me seem overly excited about going on this date," Rachel explained. "I don't want Kyle to get the wrong impression."

"And what would that be? That you're the kind

of girl who tries on half her closet before she goes out on a date?"

She shot me another look. "No. That I'm too eager."

I bit my lip to keep from smiling. "Oh. Right."

As Rachel turned around to inspect herself from the back I wondered if I should tell her how I'd seen Kyle flirting earlier at the Ocean Café. I decided against it for two reasons.

First of all, Rachel might accuse me of making it up to try and ruin her date. The last thing I wanted was another fight. Second, Kyle and Rachel had just met. It wasn't as if he was *cheating* on her or something; it was mostly just a slimy thing to do. The worst thing Kyle was guilty of was being a total flirt, which was a strike in my book but probably not in Rachel's. After all, Rachel was a total flirt herself.

"This skirt isn't long enough for night," Rachel said, mostly to herself. "I might be too cold." She flung off the dress and headed back into the walk-in closet.

It was so strange to be sitting there, in that room, getting ready to go out with Rachel. I thought back to the summer after fourth grade. Rachel had just learned to French braid and I was her hair model. I would sit in the desk chair impatiently, watching her every movement from the reflection in the mirror on the vanity.

First she'd blow my hair dry with a round brush to straighten it out. Next she'd separate it into three chunks. Then the braiding would begin.

"Ow!" I would inevitably shriek. Rachel was always pulling too tight.

"Just relax," she would respond, cool as a cucumber. "I'm making you beautiful."

I smiled at the memory.

"If you're worried about freezing, you can borrow my old gray sweatpants free of charge," I called out.

She popped her head out of the closet. "Very funny, Lauren," she said flatly.

After a few minutes of silence Rachel emerged to evaluate outfit number four.

"You'll be happy to know," she called out to me, "that I've made a decision."

I glanced up again. Rachel was standing in front of the mirror wearing white jeans and a pink scoop-neck T-shirt. Her blond hair was held back with a pink headband. I had to admit, it was my favorite ensemble so far.

"Good choice," I said approvingly.

She pretended to gasp. "Could my ears be playing tricks on me? Did you actually say something *nice?*"

I laughed. "Don't let it go to your head. Seriously, though, that's the best one yet. It's definitely not obvious."

"Good," Rachel said, heading toward the bathroom. "Now all I need is the right makeup." Rachel acted as if *Seventeen* was her bible or something. And all for a guy who probably wouldn't notice the difference anyway.

I glanced over to the clock on the nightstand. Nearly seven-forty. If we were going to get to the club on time, we'd have to leave in about fifteen minutes. Even though I had a suspicion that Rachel would want to be "casually late," I decided that now would probably be a good time for me to change too.

I got up from my seat on the bed and switched out of my bathing suit and into a long-sleeved black-and-white-striped T-shirt. Out of the corner of my eye I cast a look at myself in the full-length mirror across the room.

Ever since I was little, people have always told me that they loved my hair. Its fiery color and thick ringlets definitely make me stand out in a crowd. But to be honest, I would have much preferred to have Rachel's straight, dazzling blond locks. Not that I would ever tell her or anything.

I gave my outfit the once-over. The overalls didn't exactly hug any curves the way Rachel's jeans did, but I wasn't interested in showing off my body. I wanted to be comfortable. I wanted to do anything I could to make the night more bearable. From what I'd seen of Kyle, I figured his cousin was probably as irritatingly outgoing as he was. I wondered what he would look like. He was probably a blond pretty boy too. Definitely not my type—not that I really had one.

I guess you could say that Jonathan Groff was sort of my type. Jonathan didn't care about how he looked. He wore wire-rimmed glasses and approached everything with this intense, brooding, intellectual manner. He was mysterious. Kyle, on the other hand, was about as far from mysterious as you could get.

I looked at the mirror one last time and sighed. I had told everyone, especially myself, that I hadn't cared when Jonathan left the homecoming dance with Cori. From the way her face lit up every time he had spoken to her, it was obvious that Cori liked Jonathan more than I ever had. But the fact that Jonathan had never apologized for leaving me there like a total loser still triggered a silent fury inside me. Even now I got that sledgehammer feeling in the pit of my stomach whenever I thought about it. But as humiliating as Jonathan's behavior had been at the time, it made one thing very clear: No guy is worth looking like an idiot over. And I would never put myself in that kind of vulnerable position again.

"Okay," Rachel said, returning from the bathroom. "Ready when you are."

I shook my head, trying to rid myself of those embarrassing thoughts. "I'm ready," I said.

Rachel let out a little laugh.

"What?" I asked, frowning. "Don't tell me that no guy is going to notice me if I'm wearing overalls, because we still have a deal."

"No," she replied matter-of-factly. "I was actually just thinking how funny it was that you could care so little and still wind up looking so great."

For a minute I just stood there, totally caught off

guard. I could feel myself starting to blush. "Uh . . . thanks, Rach," I mumbled.

She gave me a crooked smile. "You look shocked."

"Well, we haven't exactly been complimenting each other all day," I said.

"No, we haven't," Rachel said in a sheepish tone. "Look, Lauren, I don't want us to spend the rest of the summer at each other's throats. It's no fun for me, and I'm sure it's no fun for you either."

I nodded, unable to think of anything remotely intelligent to say.

"So what do you say we start from scratch?" she suggested. "Let bygones be bygones. Clean slate."

I managed a little grin. "Sure." I was actually a little relieved. It was going to be awkward enough hanging out with two guys I didn't know.

"Good," Rachel said, grabbing her purse and heading for the sliding glass door. "Then let's get going!"

"Here goes nothing," I mumbled as I headed out the door behind her.


"Rachel, over here!" Kyle called out from across the deck. He laughed. "I was afraid you were going to stand us up."

Rachel giggled. "Oh, come on. We can't be more than ten minutes late."

"I guess you're right." He checked his watch, then cocked an eyebrow. "The time must have been moving slowly in anticipation."

I thought I would gag. Did Kyle own some kind of cheesy line manual or something?

"Rachel and Lauren, I'd like you to meet my cousin Jesse Shaw," Kyle said, motioning to the somber-looking guy standing next to him.

I glanced at Jesse briefly. With his short dark hair and brown eyes, he looked much less like a Ken doll than Kyle. He was taller and thinner, for one thing. And he was dressed casually—almost sloppily, with his T-shirt hanging out of his jeans. It sort of reminded me of the way Jonathan Groff dressed. In fact, Jesse was pretty cute. I felt my spirits lift involuntarily.

"It's nice to meet you, Jesse," Rachel said brightly.

"Yeah," Jesse grunted.

I mustered a polite smile. "Hi."

Jesse just nodded, avoiding my eyes. He obviously felt every bit as awkward as I did. One thing was for sure: Jesse was not the social butterfly his cousin Kyle seemed to be—not by a long shot.

"I thought we could head in to Vineyard Haven," Kyle said. "Maybe we could play some minigolf."

Aside from being the main ferry port, Vineyard Haven probably had the closest thing to a night life on the island. All the little towns on the island looked pretty similar, with quaint little streets and a variety of shops, but Vineyard Haven was my favorite. The area around Main Street had the biggest concentration of shops and restaurants, including the Martha's Vineyard staples—The Black Dog Tavern and Mad Martha's ice cream. It also had a "games" building that consisted of video games, miniature golf, and carnival-type games where you could win stuffed animals. It was probably the most touristy place on the island, but I had to admit that even with the clichéd Black Dog T-shirts and hats that every tourist bought, I liked the feel of it. It felt like summer. Just walking up and down Main Street was enough to make school seem worlds away.

"That sounds perfect, Kyle," Rachel said, looking up at him with the same goofy expression she'd worn that afternoon.

"Whatever," Jesse mumbled.

"I never turn down a round of minigolf," I added lamely, just to say something.

"Should we walk on the beach to get there?" Rachel asked. "I love walking on the beach at night."

"Great idea." Kyle beamed at her. "The moonlight looks so beautiful on the ocean."

I groaned inwardly. *The moonlight looks so beautiful on the ocean.* What was this, a Velveeta convention? I didn't know how much more I could take.

Rachel and Kyle headed down the ramp, leaving Jesse and me alone on the deck.

"Uh . . . I guess that's our cue to follow," I said, motioning in the general direction of the shore.

Jesse followed the other two down the ramp

without looking at me. "Guess so," he muttered.

I frowned. Jesse might be cute—but he was turning out to be kind of rude. *Oh, well. It doesn't make a bit of difference,* I reminded myself. *This night isn't going to last forever.* As I walked onto the beach I could feel the wind making a tousled mess of my hair. I wished I'd brought a hair clip— but what did it matter? I could live with having an unruly mop of curls on my head. At this point I could live with being completely bald. I certainly wasn't trying to impress anyone.

I found myself looking at Jesse's behind. I shook my head. So his butt looked good in jeans; big deal. I squinted up ahead at Rachel and Kyle—and saw that they were already holding hands. I almost laughed out loud. It was ridiculous. They had just *met!* Suddenly Rachel's head titled back and she let out a high-pitched squeal of delight, no doubt at another one of Kyle's dumb comments. At that point I realized that no matter how rude Jesse was, he was my only possible salvation from an evening dominated by the world's most annoying couple. I ran to catch up with him.

"So you're working at the Beach Club this summer too, right?" I began, shouting slightly to be heard over the wind and the waves.

"Yeah," Jesse replied, sticking his hand in his front jeans pocket.

"Are you a waiter also?" I asked.

He looked at the ocean absently. "No."

I waited a few moments for more of a response,

but none came. I could tell that this was going to be like pulling teeth.

"So what are you doing this summer?" I continued.

"I'm lifeguarding."

"At the pool or the ocean?" I asked.

"Pool," Jesse responded, still avoiding a look in my direction.

"Oh, a friend of mine is working at the pool this summer. Have you met Tommy Davis yet?" I usually hated to play the name game, but at least it was a source of conversation.

"Yeah. Nice guy," he mumbled.

*Well, that got me far.* "Do you get to give swimming lessons?" I didn't really care, but I felt compelled to keep asking stupid questions. I was determined to at least break the ice before we reached the minigolf course. The alternative was walking along in awkward silence and staring at the two lovebirds in front of us.

"Yeah," Jesse replied.

"Rachel and I took those lessons when we were six or something," I commented.

"Oh," he said unenthusiastically.

Finally I gave up. I'd run out of things to say. It was pretty clear that Jesse was even less interested in this "date" than I was, if that was possible. Luckily we had almost reached Vineyard Haven.

There was usually a fairly homogeneous crowd on Main Street, consisting of casually dressed families, couples, and teenagers. Most people looked slightly preppy or slightly artsy—khakis and

45

Birkenstock sandals were very popular on the island. But as we turned onto the street a large family walked out of a store. They were very loud, but what was most noticeable about them was that they were all wearing fluorescent warm-up suits—all of them, from the littlest kid to the fiftyish-looking parents—in glow-in-the-dark pink, lime green, acidic orange. The colors were almost painful to look at.

"What do you think inspired them to wear neon?" I wondered aloud.

Much to my surprise, Jesse chuckled. "I have absolutely no clue," he said.

*Finally,* I thought. For the first time that night I had received some kind of enthusiastic response. I glanced at him and decided I liked the way his brown eyes lit up when he laughed. Jesse's smile was warm and genuine, not like Kyle's annoying plastered-on toothpaste grin. It made me feel like I'd actually done something to deserve it. I was even able to relax a little bit. Before I knew it, we were at the minigolf course.

"How about Rachel and me versus you guys?" Kyle suggested.

Jesse just shrugged.

During the game Jesse and I barely said ten words to each other. Kyle and Rachel, meanwhile, spent the better part of the game giggling like some bad sitcom laugh track. My only consolation was the fact that I'd gotten two holes in one.

When we'd finished the last hole, Kyle offered to go get some sodas. Jesse reluctantly followed.

"Diet for me," Rachel made sure to chime in.

I rolled my eyes. Rachel never drank diet sodas. At least she never used to. She probably thought that by ordering one she seemed more feminine or something.

"You two seem to be hitting it off," I said evenly. I sat down beside her on a bench. As irritating as their flirting had been, I had to remind myself that Rachel and I had called a truce.

"You really think so?" Rachel asked, grinning foolishly.

"Definitely," I said. "But I think you've blown it on the not being obvious front."

"Yeah, you're probably right," she acknowledged. After a pause she added, "Jesse's cute too."

I shrugged. "He's okay."

"Just . . . 'okay'?" Rachel asked with a suggestive flicker of her eyebrows.

"Yeah. Just okay," I responded flatly, cutting her little fantasy short. Even if Jesse had been Brad Pitt, I knew that nothing was going to happen between us.

In a few minutes the guys returned, looking irritated. "Rachel," Kyle said immediately, "why don't the two of us head over to Owen Park? We can check out the view of the harbor."

She shot a quick glance at me, then looked back at Kyle. "Uh . . . you don't want to play another round?" she asked.

"I think I've lost the mood," Kyle replied, glaring at Jesse. It was the first time I'd seen him look anything but cheerful.

47

"Well . . . okay, then," Rachel said. As she rose to leave she gave me a look of bewilderment. "I guess, uh, I'll see you back at home, Lauren."

"Bye," I managed, wondering what on earth could have happened to cause such a change in Kyle. But I didn't exactly feel comfortable asking Jesse. "Well . . . what should we do now?" I asked him instead.

"Why don't we just call it a night?" he suggested.

I nodded. "Fine with me."

We headed down Main Street, once again in an uncomfortable silence. The weirdness of the scene between Kyle and Jesse had aroused my curiosity—but I was far more relieved that this night was drawing to a close. With any luck I'd never have to see either Kyle or Jesse again. After all, I'd met my end of the bargain with Rachel. I had gone out with the Shaw cousins, and now she'd have to leave me alone for the rest of the summer. I didn't even spoil her fun. No, it was fairly obvious that *her* date was going exactly as planned.

I decided to make one last effort at small talk, just to pass the time.

"So I never asked your age," I said.

"Seventeen," he responded in his usual one-word way.

"Um . . . are you going off to college this fall?"

"No," he replied, keeping his eyes fixed to the boardwalk. "Next year."

48

"Oh," I said. I grasped at any random straw of conversation. "So you're a senior?"

"Yep," he replied.

"I never know what to call myself in the summer," I said. "I mean, you've finished one year, but you really haven't started the next one yet. You know what I mean?"

Rather than nodding in agreement, or shrugging, or *anything*—Jesse just looked straight ahead.

In spite of my better judgment I started to get mad. Why was this guy going out of his way to make me feel so stupid? I was just trying to be friendly. It wasn't like he was the coolest guy in the world—or even the best looking. Well, he *was* cute, but that was beside the point. We hit the beach and kept walking in silence. I glanced up at the sky. The moon and stars had vanished behind a threatening bank of dark clouds.

"I'll be a junior," I said loudly. "Thanks for asking."

As soon as the words were out of my mouth Jesse stopped suddenly. For the first time that night he actually looked at me directly. Well, *glared* at me was more like it.

"Look, why don't you just stop it?" he said accusingly.

I took a step back, utterly stunned. "Pardon me?" I asked.

"Don't waste your time flirting with me!" he said hotly.

My mouth dropped open. *Flirting* with him! I

couldn't decide if I wanted to laugh hysterically or punch him in the face. Instead I just looked at him. "Flirting?" I shouted.

"Can't you see that it's not working?" Jesse demanded. "I mean, I've barely said three words all night. I'd think you could take a hint."

"A *hint?*" The wind was so strong on the beach that I had to use my hand to keep my hair from flying all over my face. "What *hint* is that?"

"That I'm not interested in having some kind of summer fling with you—"

"Summer fling!" I shrieked indignantly.

"Or with anyone else for that matter," he continued. "I only came tonight to get Kyle off my back."

My blood was beginning to boil. Jesse had obviously taken me for the kind of girl who only thought about having a boyfriend. The kind of girl I couldn't stand. The kind of girl . . . well, the kind of girl Rachel Hillman had become. Almost as punctuation to the anger inside me there was a flash of lightning in the sky, followed a few seconds later by a loud thunderclap.

"For your information," I hissed, "I have absolutely no interest in you—romantically or any other way."

He just smirked. "Yeah, right."

I shook my head. I couldn't believe what I was hearing. "Who do you think you *are?*" I cried. "You have a serious ego problem, you know that? You need help! So I'll repeat myself, just to get it through your thick skull: I am *not* interested in you. Not you or any other guy!"

"Well, excuse me if I find that a little hard to believe," Jesse said with a tone so smug I narrowed my eyes in disgust. "I mean, it's like you've been trying to make conversation any chance you can get."

"You're ridiculous," I retorted, just as another rumble of thunder announced that the rain was imminent.

"Ridiculous, huh?" He folded his arms across his chest. The wind whipped at his black hair. "I suppose you're going to deny now that you were even trying to *talk* to me, right?"

I snorted. "Deny that I was trying to make the best of a totally annoying, completely lame situation? No, I wouldn't *dream* of doing that, Jesse."

"Good!" he barked. "So you won't deny that you were staring up at me with those 'I'm-so-interested-in-every-word-you-say' eyes either. Maybe some guys fall for that stuff, but I'm not one of them."

At that moment the rain began to pour from the sky. It was a typical summer storm: driving, intense, and all at once.

"Fall for that stuff?" I repeated angrily. "I wouldn't care if you fell off the face of this earth, you jerk! For your information, the only reason I was even here to begin was to be polite. That's *p-o-l-i-t-e*. Go look it up in the dictionary. You obviously have no clue what it means!"

And with that I stormed off down the beach, too angry to even care that I was getting completely soaked.

# FOUR

RACHEL ROLLED OVER in bed and stretched, then blinked at me. "Hey," she said sleepily.

I had been quietly trying to make my bed in an effort not to wake her.

"Hey," I whispered. "I thought you'd want to sleep."

"It's kind of hard with all that sun," she said, squinting out the sliding glass doors that faced the beach. Sunlight was pouring into the room. The rain from the night before had long since passed.

"I can close the shades if you want to try and get back to sleep," I offered, dropping the top sheet and heading toward the blinds.

"No, that's okay." Rachel sat up in bed and stretched again. "I don't want to miss any PTH."

My eyes narrowed. "PTH?"

"Peak tanning hours."

I had to laugh. "Of course."

"Besides, I can always fall back to sleep on the beach."

"Yeah, and get your usual sunburn," I said dryly. Rachel always had a habit of letting her tanning sessions go seriously awry. My mind flashed to about a million scenes of the two of us sitting in this room with me applying aloe vera to some unreachable burned spot on Rachel's body and saying something along the lines of, "I told you so."

"I'm a big girl now, Lauren. I know how to put on sunblock. . . ." The last part of her sentence was lost in a yawn.

"What time did you get in last night?" I asked, finishing up with the bed. "I didn't even hear you come in."

Rachel's face broke into a dreamy smile, and she fell back against her pillow. "Not until after one." She sighed contentedly. "Kyle and I waited out the storm under a dock. I had no idea it had gotten so late."

I tried not to make a face. "Really?" I asked.

She giggled. "I guess it's true—time does fly when you're having fun."

"I wouldn't know." My tone was as dry as hers was glowing.

"Wasn't Kyle so . . . I can't even think of a word for him. Handsome? Smart? Funny? Amazing?"

*Try none of the above,* I thought.

"We had the most incredible time together," Rachel continued, clearly lost in her own world. "We like all the same things. We both love Hootie and the Blowfish and *Reality Bites*. And Kyle lettered in soccer and in baseball. It's like he's my fantasy guy . . . only he's real."

I resisted the urge to puke right then and there. Apparently Kyle's cheesiness was rubbing off on Rachel in a major and nauseating way. "He sounds wonderful," I mumbled, angrily marching to the dresser to find some Chap Stick. I didn't actually need it, but I figured that from my stomping to the other end of the room, Rachel would see that I wasn't at all interested in hearing about Kyle the Great.

"I can't believe it," she went on. "I've already found the perfect summer boyfriend."

I slammed the dresser drawer shut. "Break out the champagne," I said expressionlessly.

"Hey, what's up?" she asked, finally returning to planet Earth. "You seem kind of bummed. Things not work out with Jesse?"

"Yeah. You could say they didn't work out," I said. I sat down on my bed and proceeded to launch into the story about how my evening had ended, making sure to include my parting line about how Jesse should look up the word *polite* in the dictionary.

"What a jerk!" Rachel exclaimed once I had finished venting.

"*Jerk* is a nice word for what Jesse Shaw is," I mumbled.

"Well, I'm just glad that Kyle is nothing like his cousin," she said, rising out from under the covers.

"You know, I could tell right away that Jesse was bad news. I just had a sense. Didn't you?"

I shrugged. "I hadn't even thought about it, but I guess you're right."

"If you want, I'll tell Kyle when I see him again," Rachel offered.

"You've already made plans for a second date?" I asked, surprised.

"Nothing specific—yet," she answered, a hint of defensiveness in her voice. "Look, I'm sure if I talk to Kyle, he'll make Jesse apologize."

"Don't bother, Rach. I mean, I appreciate the thought—but at this point if I never hear from Jesse Shaw again, I'll die a happy woman."

"Lauren," she began. "Come on—"

"Seriously," I said firmly. "Don't worry about it." I hopped off the bed. "I think I'm going to go downstairs and get some breakfast."

I left the room without another word. As much as I knew Rachel was just trying to look out for me, she was also starting to get on my nerves. I didn't need her to meddle in my love life—or lack thereof—by getting some egomaniac to tell me how sorry he was. At this point all I wanted was to be left alone.

Mrs. Hillman was in the kitchen, making coffee. For the first time in a while I was struck by how much Mrs. Hillman looked like her daughter. Although she wore her blond hair short, it had the same bright honey color and fine texture as Rachel's. Her eyes were the same deep blue.

Looking at her mother was like staring at Rachel thirty years in the future.

"Morning, Lauren," she said with a cheery smile.

I did my best to match her expression. "Good morning."

"There are bagels in the bread box," she said, "but you might want to toast them because they're a day old."

"Thanks, but I'm not really all that hungry. I think I'll just have some orange juice."

I poured myself a glass and joined her at the table.

For a moment she just looked at me. "How are you doing, honey?" she finally asked, with that overly concerned look older people sometimes get. I'd been seeing that look a lot ever since my parents decided to split up.

"Fine," I said, cramming as much phony optimism as possible into my voice.

She sighed and patted my hand gently. "I know what's going on can't be easy for you," she said. She paused, as if she wasn't sure she should go on. "And you know, if you ask me, I think your parents are being really selfish," she added.

"No argument here," I mumbled.

"To carry on the way they have been . . ." She shook her head at some thought far off in the distance. "If the marriage isn't working, fine, it isn't working. But there's no reason for this nitpicking and bitterness. Especially when they have

56

something to be so proud of." She smiled at me. "You've really grown into an impressive young woman, Lauren."

"Thanks, Mrs. Hillman," I said, hastily taking another sip of juice. I hated terms like "young woman." It was like hearing the words "feminine protection"—it always made me squirm with embarrassment.

"Well, we're all very glad to have you here with us this summer," she said.

I nodded halfheartedly. I knew they weren't *all* happy. Rachel didn't have any other choice.

Almost as if she was reading my mind, Mrs. Hillman said, "I realize that you and Rachel haven't been as close lately . . . but I also know that she cares a lot about you, Lauren. She wants to be a good friend."

"I know," I said, sipping my juice instead of pointing out how wrong she was.

"Rachel was very upset when she heard the news about your parents," Mrs. Hillman continued.

I just kept nodding. *If Rachel was so upset,* I thought grimly, *then why didn't she ever bother to say anything about it to me?*

But I knew the answer was plain and simple. Rachel hadn't really been upset at all. Not that I could even blame her; we weren't really friends anymore. Marilyn Hillman was just trying to paint her daughter in the best light possible. My mother would have probably done the same for me.

Just then I heard Rachel's footsteps on the stairs. I put my glass down on the table and rose quickly. "Thanks, Mrs. Hillman," I muttered, heading toward the door. "I think I'm going to take a walk on the beach."

"You don't have to thank me, honey," she responded. "But don't—"

"I'll be back in a little while," I interrupted. Before Rachel even had time to enter the kitchen, I ran out onto the bright, hot sand.

After about a half hour of my walking aimlessly, hunger finally got the better of me.

I made my way back toward the house, reflecting on my conversation with Mrs. Hillman. I thought about how good it had felt to hear her say that she thought that my parents were behaving selfishly. That had been the first time an adult had truly taken my side in things. Of course, everyone was always concerned and sympathetic, but nobody had ever condemned my parents so harshly. To be honest, I was glad. They deserved it.

But I didn't buy for a minute what Mrs. Hillman had said about her daughter. If Rachel was so interested in being my friend, then why had she started off the summer by picking fights with me? Sure, things were getting a little better between the two of us, but that was just because we were each trying to make the best of a bad situation. If it were up to Rachel, I wouldn't be anywhere near this house.

I rolled my eyes as I walked through the door. Rachel was sitting at the table where I'd left her mother earlier, humming and bobbing to the beat of some song in her head and munching on a bagel. She only did that when she was really psyched about something. She was probably thinking about Kyle. I was hoping she would have already gone out on to the beach for her "PTH." But I knew I didn't really have any right to be mad—or even annoyed. We were sharing a house for the summer. We were bound to keep running into each other.

"Oh, you're back," she said, suddenly noticing me. She stopped moving.

"Yeah. I'm, uh, just going to get a little breakfast."

"Guess what?" she said brightly.

"What?" I knew I was in for more Kyle chat. Hopefully she could keep it brief.

"Kyle called ten minutes ago and asked me to go out with him again tonight."

"Great," I said, trying my hardest to keep the sarcasm out of my voice.

"We're going to the movies," she continued.

"Sounds fun." I headed for the refrigerator and pulled out some bread.

Rachel paused for a minute, looking at me. "He also said something about Jesse."

I slammed the door shut extra hard, rattling some of the jars inside. "Why would I care about *that?*"

"Kyle says that Jesse felt really bad about the way he treated you," Rachel added quickly.

"Well, he should," I mumbled.

I was just about to take the bread upstairs when the phone rang. Rachel leaped out of the chair to get it.

"Hello?" she said. "Oh. Let me see if I can find her." Covering the receiver, Rachel mouthed, "It's Jesse. He wants to talk to you."

"I have nothing to say to him," I replied, loud enough so that Jesse would hear me as well.

"Jesse, she—" After another pause she put her hand over the receiver again. "He wants to apologize."

What was this guy's problem? Couldn't he take a hint? I took two quick steps across the kitchen floor and snatched the phone out of Rachel's hand. "What do you want?" I barked.

"Look, I want to apologize for the way I treated you last night," Jesse began, sounding awkward and out of breath. "I was way out of line. But you—"

"You got that right," I interrupted harshly. I glanced at Rachel, who was staring at me with wide-eyed anticipation. My face soured, and I turned my back on her. It was bad enough being on the phone with Jesse. I didn't need Rachel hanging on my every word.

"I'm really, really sorry," he said.

"Whatever," I muttered.

"I'd like to explain why I did what I did." He took a deep breath. "You know, so that you don't get the wrong impression of me."

I hesitated. For a moment there he actually

sounded sincere. "Listen, Jesse," I finally said. "You said you're sorry. I accept your apology. You can stop feeling bad."

"I'd like to explain what happened. In person."

"That's really not necessary—"

"Well, it is for me," he stated firmly. "I know that Kyle and Rachel have plans to go to the movies tonight. Why don't we go with them? I can try to make up for what a jerk I was."

I almost laughed. Who did this guy think he was? He had to be crazy to think I'd ever want to go out with him again. "No, thanks, Jesse," I said. "I think I'll let Kyle and Rachel enjoy each other's company in private. I'd rather stay home and re-arrange my sock drawer."

All of a sudden Rachel appeared next to me. "Come with us tonight," she began whispering furiously. "Tell him you'll come with us tonight." I tried to wave her off, but it was no use.

"Lauren?" Jesse asked. "What's—"

"Jesse, could you hold on a second?" I covered the mouthpiece with my hand and glared at Rachel. "Do you mind?"

"Just tell him you'll come out with Kyle and me tonight," she pleaded in a high-pitched, whiny voice that really got to me.

"No!" I hissed fiercely. "Now get out of here!"

She didn't budge. "But I don't understand why you don't want to go out with him."

"Okay," I said as dryly as I possibly could. "I'll explain it to you. First of all, I hate his guts.

Second, going out with him won't prove a thing."

Rachel's eyes narrowed. "What do you mean, 'prove'?"

"Rachel—neither one of us is interested in dating. So why would I want to waste my time with Jesse Shaw when I'd much rather be by myself?"

"You know what your problem is, Lauren?" she said, shaking her head. "You love feeling sorry for yourself."

Anger surged through me. "What is *that* supposed to mean?" I cried.

"It means that instead of going out to the movies, you'd rather stay at home, reading and pouting and wallowing in your own misery."

"Rachel, for your information—" I broke off in midshout, suddenly remembering that my hand was still wrapped around the mouthpiece of the phone. I felt a momentary pang of embarrassment. Jesse had probably heard the whole thing. But what did I care? He was a total jerk.

"For my information *what?*" Rachel demanded.

I paused for a moment. With Jesse hanging on the line and Rachel breathing down my neck, I realized that it was foolish to prolong this argument. Neither one of them would leave me alone until I agreed to go out with them. Well, maybe it would all be for the best. I would see Jesse, tell him face-to-face that I wanted nothing to do with him, then go home and go to bed.

"For your information," I said slowly, "I'd be

happy to go out with Jesse." I uncovered the phone. "Jesse? I'll see you tonight."

"Great," he said. "So I'll see you—"

I hung up before he could finish. Rachel was just staring at me, completely stunned. I flashed her a brief self-satisfied smile, then left the room. The expression on her face almost made me feel as if I had won.

But then I remembered I had to go on a date with Jesse Shaw.

# FIVE

"I DON'T UNDERSTAND why you told them we'd meet at the club again," I said to Rachel as we headed to the Beach Club. "The movie theater is closer to the house. Now we're going in the opposite direction. We should have met them at the theater. Or at home, for that matter."

"Lauren," she responded, "sometimes you can be so thick. Meeting at the theater would give Kyle and me no time to talk before the movie, and if I'd asked Kyle and Jesse to pick us up, my parents would have given them the third degree."

"I'm sure Kyle would have passed with flying colors," I said. Judging from his silky-smooth lines, I could tell that Kyle was one of those guys who had a whole parent speech memorized. I could just hear Kyle now, telling them how he planned to study economics and international relations in college, all the better to keep up with the global markets. If it wasn't economics, then it would be political science because that was the major that law schools looked on most favorably. Anything that made him sound focused and ambitious, the perfect guy for their daughter to date.

"You really think so?" Rachel asked hopefully as she walked on beside me.

"No doubt about it," I replied. If Kyle was anything, he was smooth.

"Well, with any luck he'll meet them soon enough," she said with a smile. "If tonight is anything like last night, that is."

"The only thing I hope tonight has in common with last night is that it's over quickly," I said, not caring whether or not I put a damper on Rachel's perky spirits.

"Oh, come on, Lauren," she said with exasperation. "Why do you have to go into it with such a gloomy attitude?"

"Because last night I went into it with a positive attitude and all I got was a pile of rudeness dumped in my lap," I shot back.

"You know Jesse's sorry about what happened," Rachel continued as we stomped through the sand. "Why else would he have wanted you to come?"

"The question isn't 'why would he want me to come,'" I explained, "it's 'why would I want to go,' and, aside from getting you off my back, the answer is I don't."

Rachel let out a small groan, which I took to be one of frustration. "You are impossible, Lauren."

I decided to take that as a compliment, coming from her. "Thanks," I said.

As we continued the rest of the way to the club in silence, I wondered why Rachel cared if I went out with Jesse or not. At first I thought she was just doing it to get me riled up, but now another explanation popped into my head. She probably thought if Jesse and I hit it off, it would improve her chances with Kyle. Why else would Rachel be so concerned about my seeing Jesse?

The second we got to the club, Kyle was all over Rachel like a fly on sticky paper. After saying a quick but smiley hello to both of us, he immediately put his arm around her and turned away, leaving me and Jesse standing alone next to each other. "We'd better take off if we're going to make the movie," Kyle said as he and Rachel headed down the street in the direction we'd just come from. Jesse and I had to walk alone yet again.

*Just wonderful,* I thought. As Jesse approached me, his brown eyes shining in the moonlight, I could feel a spark rise in my chest. I swallowed hard, figuring that the sight of him had reawakened all the anger he'd caused the night before. I exhaled sharply and prepared myself for another evening with this guy. And cursed myself for agreeing to come.

"I'm really happy that you came, Lauren," he began, looking me straight in the eye right off the bat. "I have to admit that if I were you, I probably wouldn't have."

"Well, if you were me, I wouldn't have blamed you," I replied, reasoning that there was no need to be overly forgiving. "But I am curious to hear your explanation."

"And I want to give it to you," he said. "But maybe we should start walking. We don't want them to get too far ahead of us," he added, gesturing toward Rachel and Kyle.

"Okay," I said, turning down the ramp toward the road.

As we walked over the wooden planks of the ramp I was aware of how much closer Jesse was standing to me than he had been the night before. He really seemed to be going out of his way to apologize.

"It honestly had nothing to do with you," Jesse said as soon as we hit the pavement. "I mean, I barely even knew you. . . ."

"Yeah, but that didn't stop you from jumping to stupid conclusions and throwing them all in my face, did it?" After the way he'd acted, I wasn't about to make this easy for him. "And then, even after I told you that you were wrong, you still insisted that I was out to get my hooks into you or something. You have some ego."

"I guess it seemed that way," he said as the ocean winds licked at his hair, "but it had nothing to do with you. I shouldn't have said all those things to you. I should have said them to Kyle."

"To Kyle?" I remembered the tension between the two cousins when they returned from getting the soda the night before. "Does this have some-thing to do with whatever went on between you two after minigolf?"

"Sort of." Jesse nodded, averting his eyes for a moment. "See, I had no interest in going out on a blind date—no offense—and Kyle knew that, which is why he asked you along."

"You mean Kyle invited me to go out with you when he knew you didn't want to go out in the first place?" I asked, feeling a little annoyed.

"Well, yeah," Jesse said. "He knew that if he'd al-ready set up the date, I'd have no choice but to come."

"Great," I said as I turned away from Jesse's gaze and stared toward the harbor.

We were on one of my favorite strips of road on the Vineyard. There was water on either side of us, Oak Bluffs Harbor to our left, and tiny Sunset Lake to our right. Rachel and I used to try to sail minia-ture boats in Sunset Lake with the help of our fathers. I sighed at the memory.

Jesse must have interpreted my gesture differ-ently. "Don't take it personally," he continued, leaning in to tap my shoulder. "It had a lot more to do with getting me to go out with someone than with duping you. You just happened to be the first available victim."

"Now I'm really flattered," I joked.

As we walked on, Jesse let out a little laugh. "Actually there was a little more to it than that. Kyle knows that I sort of have a thing for redheads."

I stopped in my tracks. "What does that mean?"

I asked hotly. I wasn't interested in being a part of any guy's "thing." "What kind of thing?"

"Nothing," Jesse said, raising a defensive hand. He too had stopped walking and turned to face me. "Well, it's, uh . . . it's just that, well . . . my ex-girl-friend had red hair."

"Oh," I said, furrowing my brow. I found myself wondering what kind of girl Jesse Shaw would like. There would have to be more than just red hair to attract him. Then I stopped myself. What did *I* care about his taste in women?

"See," Jesse went on as we resumed our walk, "I had a girlfriend this year and we broke up a few months ago, which kind of soured me on the whole dating thing."

Something in Jesse's wistful tone had me intrigued. I wondered what had happened. "Yeah, dating can really suck," I said as I kicked a stone down the road.

Jesse looked at me with an amused expression. "Sounds like you've had your own share of negative experiences."

"You could say that." I wasn't about to go into details about Jonathan Groff and my homecoming humiliation.

Jesse stared up at the moonless sky above us. "Well, it doesn't get much worse than what happened to me."

I looked at him quizzically.

"She dumped me for my best friend. Or I should say, ex–best friend."

"Ouch," I said sympathetically.

Jesse sighed. "Yeah. I mean, I know it sounds like a total cliché. I felt like I was caught in a bad movie of the week when it happened."

I laughed. "It sounds like one."

"Yeah," he continued, "except that it was my life—and it felt pretty real when it happened."

As we neared Circuit Road I found myself surprised. Jesse and I had been walking along for a while now, and the time had simply flown by. I had to admit, I was feeling a lot better about spending the evening with Jesse. I could certainly understand how Kyle could drive him crazy, especially since I was being driven crazy by Rachel.

We continued on in silence, Jesse caught up in his thoughts and me unsure of what to say. After a few moments had passed, Jesse turned to look at me.

"Everyone seems to think another girl will take my mind off what happened," Jesse said.

"Maybe," I said with a shrug as I left the stone I'd been kicking down the road. "But I doubt it."

"Why?" Jesse asked.

"Because the same thing could happen again. Possibly even worse," I explained. "Relationships don't work out. Love is for suckers."

Jesse chuckled. "Have you told that to your friend?" he asked, motioning up the road to Kyle and Rachel.

"Yes," I said, nodding. "But it obviously hasn't sunk in yet."

"It doesn't look like it," Jesse agreed, giving me

the same warm smile I'd seen just once the night before.

"To tell you the truth," I continued, "it seems like the two of us are kind of in the same boat this summer."

"How's that?" Jesse asked.

"You know how Kyle dragged you into coming last night?" I asked.

Jesse nodded in response.

"Well," I continued, "ever since I set foot in her parents' house, Rachel has been doing the same thing to me. She just can't get it through her head that I don't want to find a boyfriend this summer."

"You too, huh?" Jesse said.

"Yeah," I answered. "As a matter of fact, the only reason I'm here right now is because she begged me to come."

"Man, I feel so stupid." He shook his head.

"Why, just because you acted like a total jerk last night?" I said teasingly.

"Well, yeah, that," he said slowly, "but also because I assumed that you were just like Kyle and Rachel. I mean, Kyle's my cousin and all—but we are *completely* different."

"Clearly," I said, "and so are Rachel and I."

"You seem like a pretty cool person," Jesse said. "And with Kyle around, I can use all the cool people I can get this summer."

"Oh, yeah?" I asked with a flattered grin as we approached the theater.

"Yeah," he answered. "I thought we could maybe start over as friends."

"Maybe," I said.

"So," Jesse asked as he opened the theater door, "do you forgive me for last night?"

"I have to admit, I actually do," I said brightly. Jesse smiled back at me in response. In the well-lit theater I couldn't help but notice the twinkle in his warm brown eyes.

We joined Rachel and Kyle, who were already in line to buy tickets.

"It looks like you two were able to patch things up," Kyle said, his arm still around Rachel. "We'll be sure to give you some privacy on the way home tonight." Kyle then gave Jesse the most obvious wink in history.

I looked over at Jesse, who barely grunted in response. I wondered who was more annoyed at Kyle's insinuation, him or me. I felt a wave of sympathy toward Jesse. Kyle, I decided, was even lamer than Rachel at her lamest. I had thought that *I* had it bad. How could Jesse take it?


"What a killer movie!" Kyle exclaimed as the four of us exited the theater into the cool night air. "That chase scene was amazing."

"I know," Rachel agreed, beaming up at him. "It totally had me on the edge of my seat."

"You have to be kidding," Jesse said. "Those things are always the same. You hit some fire hydrants, avoid some screaming pedestrians, and end up with smoke coming out from under the hood of the car."

I had to laugh. "I completely agree. But you're forgetting the one fat guy who's always so shocked and scared that he spills a milk shake all over himself."

"Right!" Jesse turned to me with a grin.

"I can't believe it," Rachel said. "Lauren, you may have met your cynical match."

Rachel hadn't necessarily meant anything by that line, but the implications of it caused both Jesse and me to look down uncomfortably.

"So where to now?" Kyle asked, putting an arm around Rachel. "I vote for some chow."

"Sounds good to me." Rachel was the first to pipe in. "I didn't eat dinner."

"I'm not hungry, but I could get something light if everyone else is," I offered.

"I'm not hungry either," Jesse said. "Why don't you guys go ahead and eat without us."

"Are you sure?" Rachel asked, shooting me a look.

"Yeah, that's fine," I said, nodding. "You two have a good dinner."

"Okay, bye," Rachel said as she and Kyle turned to walk away.

"Bye," I called back.

After a few paces Kyle turned back. "Don't do anything I wouldn't do," he said with another wink that was anything but subtle.

"What *wouldn't* you do," Jesse mumbled under his breath.

"What?" I asked, unsure if I'd heard him correctly.

"Nothing," Jesse said, dismissing my thoughts with a wave. "So what should we do now?"

"I don't know," I said, unsure if Jesse's suggestion to split up meant that he wanted the evening to end. "If you want, we can just call it a night."

"Nah. It's still early, and we *are* in town. Why not make the most of it?" Jesse shrugged. "Unless you want to get back."

"No, I don't." I blurted out my answer quicker than I would have liked.

"Great," Jesse said. He made a broad sweeping gesture with his arm. "So what are you up for? I don't know my way around, so I can't really suggest anything."

"Well, there's always Mad Martha's," I said, thinking of the Vineyard's famous ice cream chain. "Their mango sorbet rocks."

"Sounds good to me," Jesse replied. "Lead the way!"

We headed down Circuit Road, looking in the shop windows as we passed. Boutiques filled with funky crafts and ethnic-looking clothing lined the street. It was what I called "hippie-Mom" stuff, long and flowy with heavy emphasis on beads.

"Not exactly your typical beach town shops," Jesse said as we strolled along under the streetlights.

"Maybe not," I replied. "But it's very Vineyard."

"Yeah," Jesse agreed. "This is my first summer

out here, and I can definitely see that this place has a feel all its own."

I nodded. "It does."

Strolling along, I took a deep breath of that fresh island air. Jesse was right. Even the air out here had its own distinct flavor. The flavor of peace and tranquility. Of leaving your problems a million miles away.

"Where's that coming from?"

I looked at him quizzically. "What?"

"That sound."

My ears perked up. "Oh!" I exclaimed, surprising myself with excitement. "It's the carousel!"

I had almost forgotten the Flying Horses Carousel. Supposedly it was the oldest operating carousel in the country. The horses just went around and around, not up and down. But the horses, with their genuine horsehair manes and lifelike glass eyes, made up for the rather primitive ride. Rachel and I used to ride standing on the saddles, desperately trying to reach for the brass rings that hung from the top. We'd practically give our poor mothers heart attacks. But that, of course, was part of the fun. Whoever collected the most rings would get to ride again for free.

"Uh-oh," Jesse said with a devilish grin. "I think somebody wants to go for a ride."

"No, that's okay." I waved my hand dismissively. I didn't want to act like a little kid. "It's not a very exciting one. The horses don't even move."

"Well, I, for one, can never pass up a merry-go-round. Just one quick ride and then we'll get some ice cream," Jesse said, heading off in the direction of the music.

We bought our tickets and made our way onto the ride. The horses were smaller than I'd remembered. I was surprised to see how full it was. After all, it was after most kids' bedtimes. But I guess bedtimes are pretty hard to enforce over the summer.

"Lauren—over here!" Jesse called, running up ahead.

He must have found us seats. It was a good thing too. I was starting to get worried since I hadn't even seen one empty horse, much less two together. I would have felt rude suggesting that Jesse and I split up. I made my way through the other riders to find Jesse standing in between two back-to-back horses on the carousel's outer side.

"Are these okay?" Jesse asked as I approached. "They're not next to each other, but this way we can both reach for the rings."

"Perfect," I answered, climbing up on the second horse. "What good is the ride if you can't try for the rings?"

"Somehow I thought you'd feel that way." Jesse grinned as he mounted the horse in front of me.

A moment later the carousel began to move, picking up speed as it went. As we neared the front of the ride both Jesse and I leaned forward, ready to grab for the brass rings that beckoned us from their elaborate metal holder.

"Got it!" Jesse turned to me in triumph, holding his ring up proudly.

Extending my arm, I reached for the next one with focus. My fingers found the brass, and I gave it a tug. "Me too!" I cried. "It's much easier than when I was eight."

"I'll bet." Jesse grinned over his shoulder.

*He does have a nice smile.*

With the wind blowing in my hair as we continued around and around, I felt like a kid again. Maybe it was that piped-in carousel music, but something made me feel happy and carefree.

Laughing with Jesse as we neared the rings again, I realized that I was having fun. More fun than I'd had in a long time.

"You're right," Jesse said between licks of Mango Mania, "this stuff is amazing." It was a little while later, and after taking advantage of the free ride that we had both won, we had made our way over to Mad Martha's.

"That's one thing about me—I never kid about ice cream. Especially not Mad Martha's." I gestured around the crowded shop with my hand.

"I can see that." Jesse nodded as he worked on his cone. We continued eating in silence for a few moments until he changed the subject. "So, you and Rachel don't seem that tight."

"That's because we're not," I responded. "We used to be, but now we've sort of drifted apart."

"Then why are you here at the beach with her?"

Jesse asked.

"That's the six-million-dollar question," I said, rolling my eyes. "It's a long story."

"I have more than half a cone left," he said. "Fire away."

"Well." I swallowed a spoonful of sorbet. I figured I'd give him the short version of it. "Rachel's parents offered, and I didn't have much choice but to accept."

"Really? Did they chain you up or something?" Jesse asked jokingly.

"No." I laughed at the image of benign Mr. and Mrs. Hillman forcing me to do anything. "It's just that I needed to get away from home for a while."

"Oh." Jesse nodded, licking a drip of Mango Mania off his fingers. "Are your parents hard to deal with?"

"Not normally." I sighed. "But lately it's been kind of hard."

"Oh," he said again.

"They're getting a divorce."

Jesse stopped eating and looked up at me. "Oh, wow, I'm sorry. That's really tough." He sounded very serious.

"It's okay. It's not really a huge deal," I said flippantly. I didn't want this to turn into a "let's feel sorry for Lauren" conversation.

"My aunt and uncle just got divorced last year. I know it's different when it's your own parents, but I could see that it sucked pretty badly."

"Oh," I said. Usually when people try to say

comforting things about my parents' divorce, I find it grating. But Jesse looked so sympathetic, I didn't really mind.

We continued to eat in silence for a little while.

"I didn't want to spend the summer with Kyle either," Jesse said as he took a bite of his cone.

"That's fairly obvious," I said. "So why are you?"

"My dad sort of forced me into it," he explained. "He and Kyle's father, my uncle, spent all their summers here when they were growing up. So they figured it would be great family bonding for us. And then, when my dad told me I had a job at the club with housing, it was pretty hard to turn down. I mean, who wouldn't want to be out on Martha's Vineyard for the summer?"

"I obviously couldn't turn it down either," I said.

By then we had both finished our sorbet. We stood up, figuring that we should leave our valuable table to one of the many people waiting on line. Jesse and I left the bright lights of the shop and headed out of town and toward the beach.

As we walked along in the clear night air I felt no need to break our silence. Unlike the night before, the quiet between me and Jesse felt comfortable, even relaxed. It was one of the few moments I'd had since arriving at the beach where I hadn't felt at all tense.

I noticed that Jesse and I were standing so close that our shoulders were practically touching. Every so often Jesse would glance at me out of the corner of his eye. Oddly enough, it made me feel warm rather than self-conscious.

"This is it," I said when we neared the Hillmans' house.

"Nice place," Jesse commented.

"Yeah," I agreed.

We stopped walking when we got to the steps that headed up to the patio. As we stood there for a moment without saying anything, the crash of the waves seemed louder than usual.

"Well," I began as I reached for the railing, "I'm happy I came tonight."

"Yeah." Jesse nodded, "I'm glad you came too."

The relaxed quiet between us soon transformed into a textbook example of an awkward moment. Jesse was shifting his weight from one foot to the other. I had no idea what to do or say next, but I wasn't sure I wanted to say good night just yet. I found myself wondering what it would be like to kiss him.

"Well," Jesse said, breaking the silence, "I'm glad we both know that we're not into the dating thing because normally this would be the uncomfortable part."

"What?" His thoughts had startled me back to reality.

"You know, the awkward good night," he said. "I mean, we already know that we're not going to kiss."

"Right," I said a little too quickly. My heart

leaped with embarrassment. Why had I even been thinking of kissing him?

Jesse took a small step away from me. "Well, then, good night, Lauren," he said.

"Good night," I said, turning to climb the steps to the house.

"See you around," Jesse called.

"Yeah," I called back as I headed up the stairs, "see ya."

The night had worked out well. Jesse had turned out not to be the jerk I'd expected. In fact, he had turned out to be a pretty nice guy. A really nice guy, actually. A guy I could talk to.

But I still didn't want a boyfriend. And he didn't want a girlfriend.

*Yes,* I thought, *tonight had been a good thing.* Better than I could have hoped for. It'd be nice to have someone besides Rachel to hang out with this summer.

*Why, then,* I wondered as I flicked on the bathroom light, *do I feel my heart sinking?*

# SIX

"COULD YOU PASS the mustard, please?" I asked my father.

It was a beautiful, sunny day, and the club was packed. The ocean breeze tossed a stray ringlet of hair into my face. I smoothed it back and squinted into the hot midday sun.

"Dad," I repeated, "could you please pass the mustard?"

Yet again my father didn't respond. Instead he continued to stare off into the distance like he was meditating or something.

"Fine," I said, irritated. I reached across the table. "I'll get it myself, then."

I smeared mustard on both halves and took a bite into my turkey club on rye. The crunch of the lettuce seemed particularly loud, but as I glanced around the table I realized that neither of my parents had noticed. They were both sitting there on either side of me, staring off in different directions, both completely mute.

*Oh, well,* I reasoned as I fumbled for the straw in my glass of iced tea. *There are worse things than a quiet lunch.*

I took a sip of my iced tea and realized I had forgotten something. "Mom," I asked, "could you please pass the sugar?"

She gave no response but just continued sitting there in motionless silence.

I sighed. I got up and walked to the other side of the table and plucked the sugar up gingerly from the table. Once seated again I poured some sugar into my iced tea and stirred it up with the straw.

"Much better," I said after a satisfying sip.

I leaned back my head and focused on the sun's warm summer rays. This was the life—hanging at the Beach Club, no worries in sight.

But then, out of the blue, my mother began to shout.

*"Questo, quello, molto bello, bene, bene, molto bene!"* she shrieked in a high-pitched voice I'd never heard her use before.

*"Questo, quello, molto bello, bene, bene, molto bene!"* my father replied in a low baritone that sounded equally strange.

"What are you guys doing?" I gasped in horror as I turned my head from side to side, shooting them both looks of embarrassment. The whole club lunch crowd had stopped talking to stare at us.

*"Questo, quello, molto bello, bene, bene,*

*molto bene!"* my mother repeated. This time it was even louder.

*"Questo, quello, molto bello, bene, bene, molto bene!"* Dad repeated, matching her volume.

"What is with you guys?" I asked as it dawned on me that my parents were yelling at each other in opera.

*"Questo, quello, molto bello, bene, bene, molto bene!"* they belted out together in unison.

"Stop it!" I screamed, covering my ears with my hands. "I can't take it anymore!" Finally I had enough. I rushed away from the table and dove straight into the ocean. I kicked my legs and paddled my arms with feverish intensity. I had to get away from my parents.

I kept swimming and swimming, but I soon saw that I wasn't getting anywhere.

"Looks like you could use this," a vaguely familiar voice said.

I turned to find Jesse treading water next to me. He held out a blue kickboard, offering it to me.

"Thanks," I said, gratefully accepting the board. "I don't know what happened. . . ."

"I thought you might need some help," Jesse explained, putting his arms around my waist. "Just kick in nice, even strokes."

I followed Jesse's advice. In no time we were beginning to move together, out into the farthest reaches of the ocean. Gliding through the water, I felt completely at ease. I smiled as I continued to make my way through the gentle waves with Jesse's strong arms around me.

Soon we were in the middle of the ocean. Jesse and I stopped moving and met each other's deep gaze. His brown eyes began closing as he leaned in and . . .

"Lauren. Lauren, wake up."

I opened my eyes to find Rachel staring down at me.

"Rachel?" I whispered, totally disoriented.

"Hi," she said, taking a seat on the foot of my bed. "Sorry to wake you, but it's almost eleven, and you know how good ol' Marilyn can't let anyone sleep in past ten."

I rubbed my eyes and nodded. Mrs. Hillman was one of those moms who will only let you sleep until noon if you're sick. When Rachel and I were little, I never minded this, but today I could have really used some extra sleep. I had woken up feeling like someone had knocked me in the head with a hammer. Really hard. Plus I'd been having strange dreams all night.

*Oh, well,* I thought as I sat up. *Eleven o'clock isn't so bad. I should be getting up anyway.*

Rachel was still sitting on my bed.

"What's up?" I asked her in a groggy voice.

"If I show you something, do you promise not to make fun of it?" she asked.

"What are you talking about?"

"Let me get it," Rachel replied, springing up from my bed and crossing over to her own. "Look what Kyle won for me!"

She held out a big stuffed dog. It was one of those that you find at any carnival—big and pink with a little vinyl tongue sticking out of its smiling mouth.

"Isn't it cute?" Rachel was beaming. "We played about a million games at the arcade to get it."

"Adorable," I said blandly. "Must have been your lucky day."

"Ha ha," she said sarcastically as she put the dog back on her bed. "I knew you'd rag on it."

"No, I wasn't," I said, trying to sound positive. There was no reason to get into another fight—especially first thing in the morning. "I was just making a joke."

"Whatever."

"I was *kidding*," I insisted.

For a moment neither of us said anything. Rachel began fishing for something under her bed.

"Do you ever wonder why the stuffed animals that you win playing those games are so hard?" I said, thinking out loud.

"What?" Rachel asked without bothering to look in my direction.

"You know what I mean," I said, readjusting the pillow under my head. "They're cute to look at, but they're hard as rocks."

"I never gave it much thought," Rachel replied. Her voice was muffled, coming from underneath the dust ruffle.

"Or why they make pink dogs when there are no actual pink dogs in the world? Or how you end up spending ten bucks just to win some dumb thing not worth half that?"

"Lauren," Rachel said triumphantly as she pulled out a black sandal, "you can be so negative sometimes." She slipped it on and buckled the strap.

"Thanks for sharing that."

"Anyway, I had the best time with Kyle last night," she continued. The dreamy look returned to her face. "He is *so* sweet. So I don't care what you say. How did things go with you and Jesse?"

"Fine," I replied, rolling around from my side to my stomach. "Turns out that we have a lot in common."

"Really?" Rachel's eyebrows arched excitedly.

"Yeah," I said, "like the fact that neither one of us is interested in dating."

"That's too bad," Rachel said as she slipped on her other sandal, "because Jesse is really cute."

"Looks aren't everything, Rachel," I replied.

"If you say so, Lauren." She looked doubtful as she got to her feet. "I'm going back down to the kitchen. Are you coming?"

"Not for a little while," I said, lying back down. "But tell your mom that I'm up."

"Okay."

I turned over onto my back and stared up at the ceiling, listening to the sound of Rachel's footsteps heading downstairs. As I lay there in bed and thought about the dream I felt giddy and embarrassed at the same time. While the dream made absolutely no rational sense, it seemed perfectly logical at the time I'd dreamed it.

Why was I dreaming about Jesse?

It didn't take a rocket scientist to figure it out. There was no way to deny my dream—I had no control over it. Even though I'd never admit it to Rachel, a tiny part of me was attracted to Jesse.

Almost as a punishment, the image from my parents' wedding video flashed before my eyes—the two of them smiling, laughing, dancing—The Big Lie. I thought about their harsh words the day I left. I was not going to let that happen to me.

*So what if I find Jesse attractive?* I thought as I sat up in bed and stretched.

I could be attracted to someone—in this case, Jesse—but that didn't mean I had to do anything about it. Jesse was a nice guy—a really cute, nice guy—and we'd had a great time talking to each other last night. But that didn't change the facts—that love . . . or lust for that matter . . . could not be trusted.

Restlessly I pulled away the covers and got out of bed.

As soon as I was standing, my stomach rumbled. Nothing a few pieces of rye toast and a bowl of cereal wouldn't cure. Making sure my T-shirt and boxer shorts were decent enough to be seen in, I stuck my hair in a ponytail without brushing it and headed straight downstairs.

As I scampered across the cool tile of the first-floor hallway I heard Rachel's voice coming from the kitchen.

"Lauren would never admit it," she was saying,

"but I can tell that she really likes him."

I couldn't believe my ears! All I'd told her was that Jesse and I had a lot in common. *She* was the one who was all gung ho about summer romance, not me. I tiptoed closer, waiting to hear what else Rachel had to say. And who she was saying it to.

"What does Jesse do at the club?" It was Mrs. Hillman. She sounded pretty interested. Well, Rachel's mom was one of those mothers who always wants to know all the gossip.

"He's a lifeguard," Rachel informed her.

Mrs. Hillman laughed. "Lauren likes the aquatic type. Remember the crush she had on your swimming teacher? What was his name again?"

"Jeffrey Botwin," Rachel said. "He was kind of cute, in a nerdy sort of way."

"That's right," Mrs. Hillman said. "Jeffrey. She insisted on giving him every one of the toys she won at Club Day that summer. It was the sweetest case of puppy love I'd ever seen."

As I stood in the hallway I could feel a flush rising in my cheeks. How did they still remember Jeffrey Botwin?

"I think Lauren must have a thing for lifeguards," Rachel continued.

"Well," Mrs. Hillman replied, "I'm glad she's met someone nice. Maybe it'll take her mind off the divorce."

I slid my feet as quietly as possible across the hallway tiles and ran back up the stairs to the third-floor suite. Stopping only to slip on my leather thongs, I exited through the sliding glass door onto the stairs that led first to the patio and then to the beach.

I walked swiftly away from the house, heading down along the hot summer sand. The midday sun was already burning overhead, undaunted by the shore's cool breeze, but I kept going.

Jeffrey Botwin.

It was the summer that I first learned to do a flip turn in the water. The summer that Rachel and I were nine years old. At first it had been like any other summer, with Rachel and I on the Beach Club swim team. But that year, instead of Neil Abraham and his pimply back, the assistant coach was Jeffrey Botwin. In my nine-year-old opinion he looked like a movie star with his wavy brown hair and crystal blue eyes.

Even though he was seventeen, I had been determined to get him to notice me. I was forever pretending to have an injury that would require his immediate and undivided attention, but Jeffrey would always tell me to "swim it out." Finally, after missing yet another flip turn one day at practice, a lightbulb went off in my brain. Private lessons! I had figured out a way to have time with Jeffrey Botwin, the swim team god, one-on-one.

I'd demanded that my parents pay for lessons twice a week and insisted that only Jeffrey had the skills to teach me this fine aquatic art. After a lot of begging I finally got my way, and Jeffrey was all mine for two glorious half hours a week.

In a blind stupidity that only a crushed-out nine-year-old could have, I made sure to bring a present for Jeffrey to each and every lesson.

Everyone around me had known exactly what I was up to, including Jeffrey Botwin himself, but I didn't care at the time. That is, until the day Jeffrey's girlfriend came by the pool during my lesson. I can still remember the way my stomach dropped when I saw him kiss her. Suddenly, in that moment, I realized what I must have looked like to Jeffrey all along—a stupid little love-struck girl. I had never been so humiliated in my life.

But even if I had been mortified, I had to admit that my crush on Jeffrey Botwin did have its thrills. Sometimes during our lesson Jeffrey would put his arms around me to demonstrate the position that my body needed to be in to make the turns. Those thirty seconds were the best moments of my summer. In fact, I realized with a burning pang of embarrassment, Jesse had been holding me that same way in the dream I'd had the night before.

I shook my head at the thought and realized how far I'd walked. Although it seemed as if I'd only left the Hillmans' a few minutes before, I had already made it to the Beach Club.

My stomach began to rumble, reminding me that I'd left the Hillmans' without eating any breakfast. No wonder I was so hungry. I decided to go to the Beach Club and get something to eat.

I walked along the sand to the club's entrance, grateful that the Hillmans had included me on their signing privileges list. All I had to do to pay was sign my name with their membership number. Since I'd left the house with no money, there was no other way I could eat.

The club was pretty empty. It was still a bit early for lunch, so I was able to snag a prime table that overlooked the beach. I silently prayed that Kyle would not be my waiter. The last thing I felt like doing was taking the ribbing I knew he'd give me about Jesse. But I knew that he worked the lunch shift, so my chances of bumping into him were good.

I opened my menu and tried to blend in with the rest of the lunch crowd.

Just as I'd decided on a grilled cheese sandwich, I heard a voice in the distance and knew my luck had, as usual, run thin.

"Lauren." The male voice rang out from somewhere behind me. "Lauren, is that you?"

*Maybe if I don't turn around, Kyle will assume that it's not me,* I thought as I continued to stare into my menu.

But then I felt a tap on my shoulder.

Bracing myself to be friendly to Kyle against my own better instincts, I turned around and smiled brightly at . . . Jesse.

# SEVEN

"J ESSE!" I SAID, taken aback to find him rather than Kyle standing next to me. "What are you doing here?"

"I'm on a break," he answered. "I do work here, you know."

He motioned to the red tank top he was wearing. Across his muscular chest, in bold white letters, was the word *Lifeguard*. His bare arms were slim but strong. Working outside by the pool had tanned his skin to a nice bronze color. I had to fight to keep my gaze away from his incredible smile.

"Of course you do." I tried to recover. "I just didn't expect to see you."

"Didn't you hear me calling you?" Jesse asked as he grabbed the seat next to me and sat down.

"Were you calling me?" I knew that the best way to avoid a question was to ask another question.

"Yeah," Jesse said. "I was beginning to think it wasn't you."

"Well, it's me, all right," I said, "the one and only."

As I looked at Jesse, I realized that I was still wearing the T-shirt and boxers I'd slept in. I was also aware that I'd thrown my unbrushed hair up into a ponytail. In other words, my appearance was somewhat less than ideal. Very much less than ideal, actually.

I began to feel very self-conscious. But I reminded myself that what I looked like didn't matter any more at this moment with Jesse than it had as I was walking down the beach by myself. I tucked a stray curl behind my ear anyway.

"So what brings you by the club?" Jesse asked.

"Hunger, basically," I replied. "I was taking a walk down the beach and figured I'd stop by and grab something to eat." There was no reason to explain the events of this morning to Jesse.

"Well," he said, looking at his watch. "I have about twenty minutes left on my break. Do you mind a little company?"

"Not at all," I said, smiling. "So, what can you recommend?"

"Anything with cheese or chocolate," Jesse said.

"Mmmm. Sounds good," I agreed. "You must have read my mind."

I realized that this was the first time I'd seen Jesse in the daytime. I'd never noticed the way the sun brought out the golden flecks in his brown eyes. Looking into them, I felt my heart beat faster.

*What is happening to me?* I wondered.

I decided to chalk up my newfound mushiness to the aftereffects of my dream. Dreaming about someone you barely know and then seeing them less than twelve hours later is bound to cause some kind of involuntary reaction.

Jesse turned to motion for a waiter. "Have you decided on something? We'd better order soon if I'm going to make it back on time." His cheeks were flushed. I didn't know if it was from the sun or what, but noticing it made my insides feel warm.

"Yeah, but if you're in a rush," I volunteered, "don't feel like you have to stay on my account."

"That's okay," he said. "I could use a glass of iced tea. I don't eat lunch until my next break."

"Okay." I was ashamed to admit it, but I was happy that he'd chosen to spend his break with me. Too happy.

"Anyway . . . ," Jesse started.

"Hey, Jesse! You want to order something?" From out of nowhere our waitress had appeared. She pushed her curly brown hair away from her round face, smiling.

"I'm just going to have an iced tea," Jesse answered, "but I think Lauren here is getting something more substantial."

The waitress turned to look at me. Up until he'd mentioned me, her gaze was so fixed on Jesse that she hadn't even noticed I was sitting next to him.

"Hi." I smiled feebly as the waitress sized me up.

"I guess I should introduce you two," Jesse said. "Roni Jacobson, Lauren Tyler. Lauren Tyler, Roni Jacobson."

"You look really familiar," Roni said, squinting. "Do you go to Newton North?"

"No," I answered. "Newton South, actually."

"Oooh, an archrival!" Roni joked. But I could tell that she did consider me a rival—and not as a matter of school spirit.

"If you're into football, I guess so," I replied.

"Well, it's nice to meet you anyway, Lauren," Roni said in a fake, saccharine tone. Turning to Jesse, she added, "I thought you said you didn't know anyone out here!"

"Well, Lauren and I just met."

"Okay, Jesse, I'll forgive you this once," Roni said, hitting him playfully with her pen. Her little gesture made me tense up. I was not enjoying watching Roni flirt with him. "But next time you won't be so lucky, neighbor," she finished.

"Roni's bungalow is right next to mine," Jesse explained, turning to look at me.

"Is that all I am to you, Jesse?" Roni asked, pouting her full lips in mock sadness. "Just the girl next door?"

"That and my backgammon enemy," Jesse said. He gave her his killer smile.

"I beat him almost every night," Roni said. "Except for last night, when I let him win."

I managed to muster up a polite little smile. But inside, my stomach was churning. While I had been in bed dreaming about Jesse, he was playing backgammon with some other girl.

"Don't try and act all merciful now," Jesse teased Roni. "I beat you fair and square."

As the two of them went on bickering I felt a lump rise in my throat. I couldn't stand to see Roni playfully tap Jesse's shoulder with her pen or listen to her flirtatious, mock-angry voice. I was actually beginning to feel jealous.

"Well," Roni was saying, "the only way to solve this is a rematch. How about tonight, my room?"

"Let me get back to you on that," Jesse said, shooting a glance at me.

Roni frowned. "Sure," she said casually. "You know where to find me. In the meantime, Lauren, I still haven't taken your order."

Although she continued to smile, Roni's tone was chilly. It was clear her feelings toward me were less than friendly. Even though I knew that she was worrying for nothing, I did feel an odd sense of triumph.

"I'll just have a grilled Swiss on rye," I said brightly. Since I knew Jesse would leave soon, I decided that hanging around the restaurant and chatting with Roni was probably not the best idea. "Make it to go," I added.

"Coming right up," Roni said as she turned to leave.

"I didn't know you were from Newton," Jesse said after a moment.

"Yeah," I replied. "Your typical Boston suburb. Why, where are you from?"

"D.C.," he answered.

"Really?" I asked. Not a lot of people on the Vineyard were from the D.C. area, unless you counted the Clintons' two-week stay a few years back. Most people who came there were from Boston or Connecticut, with some New Yorkers here and there. "So how did you wind up here at the Beach Club?"

"My dad grew up in New Haven," Jesse explained. "He and Kyle's father used to work here during the summers. Remember, I told you last night that it's some big nostalgia thing for our dads? Sending us here this summer lets them relive the glory days."

"Parents," I said, rolling my eyes.

"Yeah," Jesse responded. "They don't have a clue."

Roni returned with our order. "One iced tea and one grilled cheese to go," she said, handing Jesse his drink and me my bag.

"Perfect timing," Jesse said as he looked at his watch again. "I've got about three minutes left on my break."

Roni handed me the guest check. As I signed my name along with the Hillmans' member number, Roni turned to Jesse. "So let me know about tonight," she said.

"Yeah. I will." Jesse got up and watched as I signed the bill.

"Bye," Roni called as Jesse and I walked away.

I must be a truly evil person because again I felt a victorious rush come over me.

"Walk me back to work?" Jesse asked as we left the restaurant.

"Sure," I said. We crossed the deck in the direction of the main pool.

"So." Jesse gave one of my curls a tug. "What are you up to tonight?"

I just looked at him and shrugged. *Where is he going with this?* I wondered.

"You want to hang out?" he asked. I may have been imagining it, but he seemed slightly nervous.

"Um, I don't know," I mumbled. My cheeks felt like they were turning as red as a summer tomato.

"Come on, why not? It's not like it's a date or anything," he added.

"But what about Roni?" I asked. "Aren't you going to hang out with her or something?"

Jesse shook his head. "Nah. She's too pushy. She put me on the spot back there."

I nibbled my bottom lip. "Well, then . . . okay. Sure."

"Cool," he said. "So we'll get some dinner or something. And I promise I won't bring Kyle with me."

I laughed, starting to feel relieved. "And I won't bring Rachel." *It'll be fun,* I told myself. I did like hanging out with Jesse. There was no reason to stay home like a hermit just because I didn't want to fall in love. And when I considered the alternative— him playing backgammon with Roni all night—my mind was made up.

"It's a deal," he said, flashing me yet another one of his amazing grins.

While we made a plan for Jesse to pick me up at the Hillmans' at eight, I felt a pebble in my left thong.

"Hold on a second," I said, slipping off the thong. "I've got something in my shoe."

I knew that Jesse was in a rush to get back to work, so instead of shaking out the sand and putting my shoes back on, I decided to walk the rest of the way barefoot. The pool was just down the set of stairs ahead, and I'd be back on the beach soon enough.

The warm breeze felt good on my face as we continued down the steps to the pool. The beach was so pretty in the late morning sunlight.

Suddenly I felt a sharp pain on the bottom of my right foot. "Ouch!" I cried out. I sat down on one of the steps to examine my toe.

Jesse sat down next to me. "What is it?" he asked.

"It's a huge splinter," I said unhappily. "Just my luck too. I take two steps on a wooden deck, and I immediately get a splinter."

"Let me see it," he said, reaching for my foot.

"That's okay; you don't have to."

He smiled. "Come on, Lauren, it's not a big deal." He took my foot in his hands. "I promise I'll be gentle."

"Okay," I said. I knew that I was being a baby about my splinter—but I really hated them. When I was little, Mr. Hillman would patiently pull splinters out with a pair of tweezers while Rachel would try to distract me.

I watched Jesse examine my foot, and I almost felt relaxed. He was so cute in his red lifeguard shirt and his dark brown hair curled sweetly around his ears. One of his fingers tickled my foot, and I pulled it away. "Sorry." I giggled. "I'm kinda ticklish."

"So I see," he said as he took my foot in his hand once again. "Now relax. It's just a little splinter."

"*Little?* You call that thing little? It's huge!"

Jesse stopped looking at my foot and looked up at me.

"Okay." I smiled. "So I have a small phobia of splinters."

"Well, you have nothing to fear; you've got Dr. Shaw here with you." He gently put my foot down and massaged my shoulders to relax me. It wasn't working. Instead of feeling relaxed, I felt chills go through me as his hands released the tension in my neck. I was getting goose bumps. I hoped he didn't notice.

"That feels . . . good," I said shyly.

"Good." He stopped massaging me and pulled a Swiss Army knife out of his pocket. "Good thing you're with a lifeguard—we're prepared for any emergency." Then he pulled my foot back toward him and began to use the tweezers on the knife to pull out the splinter.

I watched as he carefully maneuvered the splinter out of my foot. His face was all seriousness and concentration. I couldn't help thinking how cute he looked with that intense expression on his face. And he smelled great. Like coconuts and pineapples. A warm summer smell.

"I almost got it," he whispered.

I leaned in to get a better view. My heartbeat quickened as I realized how close our heads were. I tried to retain some sense of composure. *Just stay calm, cool, and collected,* I told myself.

But I was sure that I had goose bumps now. I forgot all about the splinter as our heads continued to move closer and closer. . . .

"Got it," he said, holding up the chip of wood in the tweezers. He looked up at me, and suddenly we were staring into each other's eyes.

"Thanks," I whispered. Our noses were practically touching. My heart was doing somersaults in my chest.

"No problem," he said quietly, tilting his head.

The next few moments felt like they were happening in slow motion. Without any thought I met Jesse's lips and we began to kiss. It was soft and passionate at the same time, and I felt as if fireworks were going off in my stomach. In short, it was amazing.

"Jesse," I said, pulling away. Jesse was strictly a friend. I didn't want us to start something I knew we couldn't finish.

"I—I'm sorry," he said as he quickly stood up. He took a step back, away from me. "I just got carried away."

"Yeah, me too." I averted my eyes. I knew that one look at Jesse would destroy all the self-control I'd just regained.

"So, uh . . . are we still on for tonight?" Jesse asked awkwardly.

"Um . . . r-right. Well . . . um . . ." I didn't trust my voice to say anything more. I knew I *didn't* want something like that to happen again. It was *exactly* what I didn't want. But I wasn't sure I could trust myself not to let it happen again. Especially since part of me, the physical part, hadn't wanted to stop kissing Jesse. Ever.

"I don't know, Jesse," I said, slipping on my sandals and rising to my feet. One thing was certain, I had to get away from him as soon as possible. I limped down the steps, nursing my sore foot while quickly trying to put distance between us. "I'll call you later," I said over my shoulder.

I *would* call him. I just didn't know what I would say.

# EIGHT

M Y MIND WAS spinning as I sat down on the
sand. It was a weekday, so the beach was
fairly empty. Thankfully, Jesse hadn't followed me
away from the pool deck. I needed to do some
clearheaded thinking. Alone. The last thing I could
take was having Jesse nearby.

*How could I have let that happen?* I wondered
as I ran my fingers through the warm sand.

I had done exactly what I'd promised myself I
wouldn't. I had ignored all rational thought and let
my attraction to Jesse take control. Against my better judgment and common sense, I had kissed him.
And worse still, I had enjoyed it. *A lot.*

I shook my head at my own stupidity. Why did I
let him sit down and talk to me? Why did I agree to
walk him back to work? And why, for heaven's
sake, had I let him take out that splinter?

Everything had been under control until then.

Sure, I had felt a little spark when Jesse had asked to hang out with me, but it was nothing I couldn't handle. That is, until he leaned down over me and held my foot in his strong, gentle hands. . . .

What was I going to do now?

*Way to go, Lauren,* I thought as I shook my head ruefully. *You've managed to make your life a total disaster.*

I looked down at my lap and realized that I still had the sandwich I'd ordered. Yum. It was probably a gooey mess by now. But maybe some of my light-headedness was caused by hunger and not by Jesse's kiss. I opened the takeout bag and fished out my grilled cheese on rye.

As I bit into the sandwich I almost had to laugh. Here I was, sitting on the beach in my pajamas, eating a soggy sandwich and hoping that the strong sun wouldn't burn my unblocked skin too badly.

And who said summer vacation wasn't fun, fun, fun?

I continued to gulp down my cold grilled cheese sandwich and tried to console myself with the possibility that my unkempt appearance would get me off the hook with Jesse. Maybe when he had a little time to think about it, he'd remember how terrible I had looked and he'd never want to kiss me again.

The prospect, while making me laugh to myself, left me feeling strangely deflated.

I was taking my last bites when my thoughts were interrupted by a sudden distraction. From out of nowhere a beach ball dropped into my lap. It was one of those bright, blow-up kinds. I picked it up and tried to figure out who it belonged to.

I didn't have to look far. A woman holding a small child by the hand approached me.

"Is this yours?" I asked, holding up the ball.

"Actually it's my daughter's," the woman said with a smile. "Amy, there's the ball. Go say thank you to the nice lady for taking care of it."

The girl stood silently on the sand, sucking her thumb. She couldn't have been more than four years old. She was definitely still in the shy phase.

"Here, Amy," I said, holding out the ball for her to take.

She grabbed the ball out of my hands and ran awkwardly back to her mother's side.

"I hope we didn't bother you," the woman said. Another little girl of a similar height ran up to where they stood. Her blond curls blew in the breeze.

"It's no problem," I replied.

"Say thank you, girls," the mother said, looking down at her daughter's now-calm face.

"Thank you," they said in unison.

"You're welcome," I said.

The woman walked back in the direction she came, the girls running in front of her, holding hands. I watched as they stopped at their blue-and-white-striped blanket. A man was standing and waiting for them to return. As soon as they approached, Amy threw the ball to the man and he caught it. He smiled and tossed the ball back to the child. I could hear her squeals of delight in the distance.

I stared at Amy with envy. Not so long ago I was a little girl just like that, playing with my mom and dad. Back then the worst thing I could imagine was losing a beach ball. Now my parents were on their way to divorce court, and I'd managed to create even more problems for myself. Feeling my eyes tear up, I wished that somehow, some way, I could go back to that carefree time.

And back then I'd had my own little blond-haired companion. What had happened to Rachel and me? We'd been getting along a lot better, but somehow we still weren't clicking. I guess our friendship was too far gone to save. Just like my parents' marriage.

Sniffling, I tried to regain my composure. Getting jealous of toddlers wasn't going to help things. Instead of sitting around and making myself sad, what I needed to do was to make some decisions.

The first of which was what to do about Jesse. I didn't know whether I should risk it all and go out with him that night. I had promised to call him with my answer.

My first instinct was to simply say "no." Seeing Jesse again would only be tempting fate, as our encounter at the club had just proved. Something was bound to happen, something that would make me cross the line of friendship into romance. Yes, it would definitely be easier to resist Jesse by avoiding him.

I looked out across the ocean waves toward the horizon. It was really too bad. Jesse was the first person in a long time who I could actually relate to. And given the fact that the only other people I knew on the Vineyard were Rachel, Kyle, and Tommy Davis, I was acutely aware of how much I needed a friend. The hot midafternoon sun blazed on my face, and I felt another pang of sadness come over me.

*If only I had someone to else to talk to,* I thought, *maybe Jesse's friendship would be easier to give up.*

"What are you doing here?"

My shoulders sank the moment I heard Rachel's voice from behind me.

"I'm sitting on the beach," I replied, turning my head to meet her gaze. "It's a pretty common activity," I added, motioning to the other people on the beach.

"Yeah," Rachel responded, tucking a stray hair behind her ear, "but I don't see any of them wearing their pajamas."

I sighed deeply. The morning had been rough enough already, thanks in part to Rachel and her mother ragging on my childhood crush.

"Then I guess I'm really making a fashion statement," I said, wishing that she would just leave me alone.

Instead Rachel stepped forward in her yellow halter top and cutoff jean shorts and sat down next to me on the sand.

"I'm on my way to the beach club to see Kyle," she said in the dopey voice that she reserved for discussions of her favorite waiter. "He asked me to stop by on his lunch break."

"Good for you," I said, trying to muster up some peppiness.

"Why don't you come with me?" she asked. "You could stop by the pool and see Jesse." She winked.

I rolled my eyes. "Rachel, get out of your fantasy world," I said. "Jesse and I are just friends."

I told myself that despite what had happened at the club earlier, it was still technically the truth.

"Have it your way, Lauren," Rachel replied in a jokey, singsong voice, "but I know you're into Jesse, even if you can't admit it yet."

I was getting sick of her teasing. After the kiss I'd shared with Jesse, it kind of hit a nerve. "Can't you just leave me alone already? Go find Kyle and work on your own love life."

I stood up and brushed the sand from the seat of my boxer shorts. Maybe the silent treatment could get her once and for all to mind her own business.

Without saying another word, I began to walk inland toward the street.

"Whatever you say, Lauren," Rachel called from behind me. I didn't bother to turn back.

I could feel the hot sand finding its way back into my sandals as I continued to walk, but I wasn't stopping to shake it out. I was too preoccupied by thoughts of how to save myself from a whole summer's worth of Rachel's pestering.

As I climbed the concrete steps that led from the beach to the paved dead-end street, I came to an important conclusion. Kiss or no kiss, I needed a friend. I needed Jesse.

I knew exactly what I had to do.

The clock on the wall read two o'clock as I entered the main pool gate. I had no idea what his work schedule was like, but I hoped that Jesse wasn't in the middle of a swimming lesson.

I knocked on the white-slatted office door. Seconds later I heard footsteps inside, moving toward the door.

"Can I help you?" a very tan blond guy asked as he peered out the doorway. He had zinc oxide on his nose and was wearing a red lifeguard tank top identical to the one that Jesse had worn.

"I hope so," I said. "I'm looking for Jesse Shaw."

"He's in the chair at the shallow end." The guy pointed out toward the pool.

"Thanks," I said.

I walked past the clusters of lounges toward the lifeguard chair and hoped for the hundredth time that Jesse wasn't offended by the way I'd rushed off earlier. As I neared his chair I looked up at him.

He was perched at least six feet off the ground with a whistle hanging from his neck, looking strong and confident. His tan, muscular shoulders rippled under his rolled-up T-shirt. His dark hair was tucked underneath a baseball cap and his brown eyes were hidden behind his sunglasses, but as I gazed at Jesse, I still felt attracted to him. Definitely my type.

"Hey," he said, giving me a big smile as I approached.

*Guess he's not offended,* I thought with relief. "Hi," I replied. I had to cup my hand over my eyes to block out the sun when I looked up at him.

"I didn't expect to see you here." Jesse had to bend down to talk to me. I was standing under him, leaning against one of the poles of the lifeguard chair.

"Well, I told you I'd get back to you, so . . ."

"Listen, Lauren," Jesse began before I could go on, "I want to apologize for what happened before—"

I held up my hands. "Wait. Stop. You don't have to apologize. Let's just say that we both lost our heads for a minute and leave it at that." The truth was, I didn't want to discuss our kiss in detail. I just wanted to move on, as friends.

"Yeah." He nodded. "I agree. Things just got a little out of hand for a moment. But that shouldn't stop us from being friends."

I breathed a sigh of relief. It was so good to know that we felt the same way. "Right. We'll pretend it never happened—a clean slate."

"So does that mean we're still on for tonight?" Jesse raised his eyebrows, looking hopeful.

"Sure, as long as we agree that it's not a date," I said. "Because it seems pretty clear that we should just be friends, right?" I didn't know who I wanted to convince more, Jesse or myself.

"Absolutely," Jesse answered, his amazing grin widening. "No date."

"Great," I responded, matching his smile with my own. "Then I'll see you later."

"Yeah, I'll come over around eight," he said.

I turned to leave, feeling confident about my decision. There was no way that anything other than a friendly good time was going to happen with Jesse that night.

"Lauren?" Jesse called out.

I stopped and turned around to face him from the other side of the pool.

"I'm, uh, really glad we'll be seeing each other tonight," he called.

"Me too," I said. And I meant it.

# NINE

"THE HILLMANS SEEM pretty cool," Jesse said as we walked off the patio and onto the beach early that evening.

"Yeah," I answered, "they are."

"So," Jesse continued, "what do you want to do?"

"I don't know." I looked around the beach. "It's so beautiful out tonight . . . we definitely need to do something outside."

It was that time of evening when the sun fades enough to leave only a handful of beachgoers on the sand but hasn't yet turned the sky to pinkish orange. I had figured that Jesse and I would probably grab a bite to eat together, but it was still too early for that.

"We're kind of near that place that rents in-line skates," Jesse pointed out. I could tell from his tone that he really wanted to go there.

"No way." I shook my head. "I can't skate to save my life."

"That's perfect," he replied enthusiastically. "Neither can I."

I stopped walking and turned to face Jesse. "Then why should we rent skates?"

"Think about all the pedestrians we can scare," he said, stopping to meet my perplexed expression with his killer smile. "It'll be like the blind leading the blind."

I got a mental picture of us swerving uncontrollably through terrified crowds. It *was* a funny image. But falling on my butt repeatedly wasn't exactly my idea of a good time.

"It sounds kinda fun," I admitted, "but I'd rather stay in one piece."

"Then we'll wear all the protective gear we can find," Jesse persisted. "Even those goofy-looking knee pads."

"I don't know . . . ," I began.

"C'mon, Lauren," Jesse said, elbowing me playfully, "where's your sense of adventure?"

"All right, all right," I acquiesced, giving him a little shove. "But we have to promise not to laugh too hard at each other."

"I promise," Jesse replied, holding his hands as if he were swearing on a Bible, "no laughing *at,* only *with.*"

"Good," I said, resuming our leisurely pace but turning now in the direction of the street rather than the beach.

As we walked together I couldn't help but notice how many couples there were—holding hands, hugging, acting blissfully happy. *All these romances will be over before the summer ends,* I predicted.

I caught a glimpse of Jesse and me in a store window reflection. Jesse looked especially cute in his beat-up old jeans and a gray faded Georgetown T-shirt. I was wearing a pair of jean shorts and my favorite worn-out dark green sweatshirt. My curly red hair was wild as usual. I smiled to myself, realizing that Jesse and I *did* look like a couple made for each other, neither of us really caring what we wore. Rachel and Kyle were so overly concerned about their appearances, making sure to wear all the latest trendy clothing. But Jesse and I looked totally relaxed.

"What are you thinking about?" Jesse asked as we neared the rental place.

I was so lost in my thoughts, I hardly heard him at first. "Oh, nothing." I shook my head, trying to pull myself back to the present. "I was just wondering why so many couples seem to appear in the summertime."

Jesse smiled. "Yeah, I noticed all those couples too. But who knows if they actually are. We probably look like we're going out too."

I looked up at him, surprised.

He rolled his eyes. "All I meant, Lauren, is that some of those other people could be like us, just friends."

"I guess you're right."

"I usually am," he teased. "Look, here's the rental place." He pointed to a small shack, and we went over to the counter to rent skates. After we exchanged our shoes for skates, we walked over to a bench to lace up.

"I don't know how I let you talk me into this," I muttered as I flung the straps of my minibackpack over my shoulders. "I know I'm gonna fall flat on my face."

"Then I'll peel you off the sidewalk," Jesse said reassuringly.

"Why are you so excited about doing this?" I asked, looking at the back of his head as he bent over to adjust the tongue of his left skate. "This is bound to be just as hazardous to your health as it is to mine."

"Because I've wanted to learn to skate for a long time," he said, lifting his head to face me. "All my friends are so good, I could never keep up with them. I don't want to embarrass myself by trying to learn with one of them."

"To tell you the truth, that's why I haven't learned yet myself," I said.

"Well, then, I think we've found ourselves a mission," Jesse said. "If we consider this our first lesson, by the end of the summer we'll both be pros."

Jesse's killer smile brought butterflies to my stomach. I tried to tell myself that it was just nervousness about skating.

"Let's see how it goes today before we make a

summer-long commitment," I cautioned as we rose from the bench. For all I knew, we could both end up with broken arms.

"Have fun," the short-haired girl from behind the counter called as Jesse and I made our ungraceful attempt to exit the shack on wheels.

"We'll try," I tossed back feebly, nearly tripping on the step leading down to the sidewalk.

"Look out, Martha's Vineyard, here we come!" Jesse hooted. He sped down the sidewalk in excitement, leaving me to wobble along, trying to catch up to him without losing control of the wheels under my feet.

Once I caught up to him, Jesse and I decided to play it safe by sticking to the quiet back roads of the more residential streets. The expert in-line skaters lined the wooden planks of the ferry dock, but neither of us felt ready to take on the challenges of the traffic and the bumpy terrain.

The dying sun shone so brightly that I had to cup my hand above my eyes for fear of being blinded by it, but gradually I became more sure of my coordination and, after a little while, actually began to relax.

"How are you doing?" Jesse called, slowing down to skate beside me.

"Not too bad," I replied happily, turning to give him a quick grin. "How 'bout you?"

He gave me a thumbs-up. In the glow of the fading sun I couldn't help but notice how attractive Jesse was. All of those feelings that I'd had when

117

we'd kissed that morning were coming back to me. Before I knew it, I started to lose my balance. I had gotten so distracted by Jesse that I wasn't paying attention to my skating.

"Whoa!" I cried, flailing my arms, trying to keep from falling.

"Lauren!" Jesse called out in alarm as he glanced in my direction.

Luckily my flapping had prevented an all-out fall, but I was annoyed at myself for getting so lost in my thoughts, especially thoughts that made my insides go to mush.

I stopped skating and leaned against a fence to gain my composure. Jesse skated over next to me. "That was a close call, huh?" he said. His eyes were staring into mine, filled with concern.

"It sure was," I said softly.

Closer than he knew.

One sunset, two falls, and countless near crashes with telephone poles later, Jesse and I returned our skates to the rental shop.

"We weren't too bad," I commented with pride as we exited the store.

"So does that mean this is the first of many skating sessions?" Jesse asked.

"If you're not afraid that I'll end up skating rings around you," I joked mischievously.

"I'm willing to take my chances," Jesse responded with a grin.

"So where should we eat?" I asked as we

stopped at the corner, waiting to cross the street.

"I don't know, but I'm starving," Jesse said.

"Me too."

"I think we're pretty near Stefano's. . . ." Jesse's voice trailed off suggestively.

"Perfect," I said. Stefano's was practically a Vineyard institution, known for its amazing thin-crusted pizzas.

We walked toward the restaurant, making our way along the town streets in the cool night air.

"I can't wait to have my first Stefano's pizza of the summer—I dream about this pizza." I sighed dramatically, pretending to be overcome by emotion.

Jesse laughed. "It *is* awesome. But there's this place in New Haven that has even better pizza."

"Better than Stefano's?" I arched one eyebrow. "I find that hard to believe."

"It is—I swear. This place was like the first pizza place in America," he insisted. "I go there whenever I visit my grandparents."

"Really? Well, I guess I'll have to make a trip there and taste for myself," I said.

"It would be worth it," Jesse said as he opened the door to the restaurant.

Stefano's was packed. The small wooden tables were crammed with both weekenders and Vineyard summer residents. I looked around at the waiters, smiling in recognition at many of them. It was a real family-run restaurant, and everything about it stayed the same year after year. The walls were covered with photos of Stefano's family and loyal customers. I saw Stefano himself, a sixtyish, chubby Italian man, walking around the restaurant with his apron on. On some nights Stefano would even play the piano, making the customers sing along with him.

"Two for dinner?" Stefano's wife asked us at the door.

"Yes," Jesse answered. "Do you think it will be a long wait?"

"No, not too bad." She shook her head. Then she just stood there for a second, looking Jesse and me over. "First date?" she added with a little wink.

Jesse and I looked at each other awkwardly for a minute, and then we both broke out into smiles.

"No," I said, "we're just friends."

"Oh, I see," she said with a smile. A smile that told us she didn't believe a word of it.

"So what do *your* parents do?" Jesse asked as he poured himself a glass of cream soda from the pitcher we'd ordered. He had just finished telling me that his parents were both trial lawyers.

"My dad's an orthodontist and my mother's a producer for the local news," I answered.

"Cool," he replied. "Two totally different careers, huh?"

"Yeah," I agreed. "It's no wonder they have nothing in common anymore."

"I didn't mean it that way," Jesse said.

"I know you didn't," I said, holding up my

hand. "I guess I was just giving you a taste of my dark sense of humor."

"I like a girl with a dark side," he said, taking a sip of soda.

"Good," I replied, "because you're stuck with one at least until the end of dinner."

"Hopefully it'll be for much longer than that," Jesse responded. The way he looked when he said it made my heart do a little flip.

But more than that it made me nervous. What did he mean by that? How was I supposed to reply? *Relax, you're reading too much into it,* I scolded myself.

Luckily our pizza came and I didn't have to say anything at all. For the next few minutes I concentrated on eating, ignoring all the confusing feelings rushing around my head.

"So here's a question I've been dying to have answered since I was about six years old," I told him a little while later, picking at the inside of some leftover pizza crust.

"That's a lot of pressure," Jesse said, furrowing his brow. "Maybe you shouldn't ask me. I'm bound to disappoint you."

"No, you won't," I told him with a laugh. "You definitely know the answer."

"Okay, then." He lifted his glass to take a sip of water. "Shoot."

"Is living in the staff bungalows as totally amazing as I always imagined?"

Jesse laughed. "Definitely not. For one thing,

they're about as narrow as a shoe box."

"Really?" I asked.

"Yes. And the showers are always running out of hot water."

"I knew it." I shook my head. "That just proves that everything you think is so cool when you're a little kid actually turns out to be lame."

"I wouldn't say that the bungalows are lame," Jesse countered, tilting his head to one side. "It's kind of fun living with a bunch of people your own age. On the one hand, everyone's there to have a good time, but it also means that everyone's constantly looking for their big summer romance."

"Oh." I nodded, thinking of Roni the waitress and her backgammon game.

"Except me, of course," he added.

"Of course." I was playing with my soda straw, wrapping it around my finger.

"You know, it's kind of funny," Jesse said.

"What is?"

"That one of the main things we have in common is that neither of us wants to date anybody," he said, leaning back in his chair.

"Right," I prodded.

"Well, in our attempts not to date anybody, we're making people think that we're dating each other." He motioned over to Stefano's wife, who was glancing at us every so often as she talked animatedly to a couple at a nearby table.

I smiled. "I guess that is sort of ironic."

"Exactly," he said as the waitress came over to set our bill down on the table.

Our hands brushed as we both reached for the check at the same time, and I felt a shiver creep all the way up my arm. *Don't be ridiculous*, I told myself. *Just because other people think we're a couple doesn't mean that we should be.*

# TEN

"DID YOU GET some good pictures this morning?" Jesse asked two days later when I came by the pool to visit him.

"Yeah, I think I got some killer shots by the pier." I had woken up early that morning to take photos of the sunrise. "You should come with me sometime—it's so beautiful."

Jesse shook his head, smiling. "I don't wake up that early. In fact, I can't believe that *you* wake up that early."

"It's so peaceful that it's worth it," I argued. "The beach is best at sunrise."

"Well, since your photos are so good, I'll admire them instead," he said.

"You're lazy," I teased him.

"Sometimes. Speaking of which," he said, looking down at his watch, "my break's over. I gotta go back to work." He motioned to the lifeguard chair.

"Okay." I stood up from the lounge chair we had been sitting on. "Enjoy the rest of your day."

"I will," he said, standing up next to me. "Hey, do you want to do something tonight?"

"Um, tonight?" I hesitated. In spite of the fact that Jesse and I had been hanging around the club and the beach like old buddies for the past two days, I wasn't sure another evening alone together was such a great idea. I was scared of reawakening all those feelings that had been stirred at Stefano's.

"Yeah. I thought we could rent a boat or something," he explained.

"I don't know. . . ."

"Aren't you the one who keeps telling me that the best way to see the night sky is on a boat?" Jesse challenged. "I'll even do the rowing."

I sighed. How could I just turn down his offer for no good reason? It would be fun. All I had to do was keep those feelings at bay.

"You're on," I said, smiling.

"Cool," he said. "Listen, it's going to have to be a little later tonight. Kyle's parents are visiting, and I have to have dinner with them."

I wondered if Rachel would be joining them.

"No problem—when do you want to go?"

"Around nine, nine-thirty? I'll come by the Hillmans' to get you when I'm ready." He was already walking back toward the lifeguard chair.

"Just don't eat too much," I called after him. "We wouldn't want to tip the boat!"

"I'll try to control myself." He laughed and kept walking.

"Are you sure you don't want anything to eat? There are plenty of leftovers downstairs," Rachel asked me as I was getting dressed that evening.

"No, I'm not hungry, thanks," I answered, rummaging through my drawers. I'd had a really late lunch and didn't feel like eating.

Looking up, I noticed Rachel sitting on her bed, watching me. She didn't look as though she had any plans to move.

"Kyle's parents are in town," she said in her "isn't he the greatest?" tone of voice.

"That's nice," I mumbled, finally finding my white T-shirt.

"Yeah." She rolled over on her back and stared up at the ceiling. "He went out for dinner with them tonight—with Jesse too, actually. Hopefully I'll get to meet them tomorrow."

"Yeah. Jesse told me." I pulled on a pair of black leggings—I figured the leggings would be good for boating. There was always some excess water in those rowboats. If the leggings got a little wet, they'd dry much faster than jeans. I was coaxing my hair into a barrette when Rachel sat up and looked at me with a strange expression on her face.

"I've never seen you spend so much time in front of the mirror," she said. "Where are you going anyway?"

"Nowhere," I answered, "just rowing."

Her eyebrows arched. "With Jesse?"

I nodded casually and tried to ignore her.

Rachel stood up. "I see," she said teasingly.

I rolled my eyes. "We're just friends. That's all."

"Oh." She smiled. "Then why are you bothering to fix your hair?"

"Because," I said in an exasperated voice, "it's annoying when it gets in my face when it's windy. It makes it hard to see."

"Right. Of course," she said. She obviously didn't believe me. "You know what I think would look good?" she added.

I turned to face her. "What?"

She pulled some strands of my hair out of the barrette so that a few stray curls fell around the sides of my face. "There, that looks great."

"Whatever," I mumbled. But when I looked in the mirror, I *did* like how my hair looked. "You know, Rach, that *does* look better. Thanks. I mean, not that I really care . . ."

"You're welcome." Rachel beamed triumphantly.

The doorbell rang at that moment, saving me from any more of Rachel's "I know you like Jesse" comments. "That's Jesse—gotta go," I said. I grabbed my wallet and ran out of the room.

As I ran down the steps I tried to convince myself that my excitement was just the relief I felt at escaping Rachel's taunts.

★   ★   ★

127

"So now we've done skating and rowing," I said to Jesse as we rowed back to return the boat. "What's next—fishing or skeet shooting?"

"I'd say we should work on the skating before we move on." Jesse was smiling. It was dark, but I could still see his face under the dock lights. "I was starting to feel like a pro the other night."

"Let's not get all cocky," I warned. "We still had a few near-misses there."

Jesse's muscles rippled as he eased back the oars. He was wearing a short-sleeved oatmeal-colored thermal shirt that showed off not just his muscles but his healthy lifeguard's tan.

"Don't start doubting our abilities now," Jesse teased. He was rowing backward, facing me as he talked. He looked really cute with his hair all tousled from the wind.

"Hey, pro, watch out—you're going to steer us right into that boat." I laughed as Jesse stopped, startled, and turned around. We were right in front of the dock. We jumped out of the boat and pulled it up onto the sand.

"You guys made it just in time," the guy at the rental place called to us. "I'm just about to close up."

"Close?" I said. "What time is it?"

Jesse looked down at his watch. "Wow, it's five to eleven. I had no idea it had gotten so late."

"Me either." Jesse hadn't picked me up until about nine-thirty, and we had completely lost track of time. I suddenly felt a rumbling in my stomach. I had forgotten about eating dinner too.

"Hey, I'm starving. Let's go get something to eat," I suggested once we had paid for the rental.

"What do you feel like?" he asked.

"I don't know." I furrowed my brow. "What do you think is open now?"

Jesse was silent for a moment, looking at the ground thoughtfully. "I got it. How about Barry's Burritos? I think it stays open till midnight."

I gave him a big smile. "Great idea. I love that place."

The restaurant was actually just a colorful shack, and it did great business because everyone loved their burritos, tacos, and nachos. And it was open late in order to satisfy the hungry college kids as they spilled out of the bars.

Luckily the line wasn't too long, and in minutes we each had a large burrito, overflowing with beans, rice, cheese, and chicken. We grabbed two empty lounge chairs and sat by the water, ready to dig into our Mexican feast.

"Didn't you eat dinner with Kyle's parents?" I asked Jesse, unwrapping my burrito.

"Well, yeah," he said in between sips of his soda. "But that was hours ago. I worked up an appetite from all that rowing. Anyway, I can never turn down a Barry's burrito."

"I know what you mean." I took a big bite, savoring it. "Hey, aren't you going to tell me that you know a place in New Haven that makes even better ones?"

He smiled, and under the glow of the moon I could see his eyes twinkling. I felt a warm rush of emotion go through my body.

"No," he said, "but there is this place in California. . . ."

I laughed, tracing my feet in the sand. I loved the feel of the cool, soft sand on my toes.

I had finished eating and was looking up at the night sky when I felt Jesse's gaze on me. I turned to face him. "What is it?" I asked. I looked into his warm brown eyes, and my pulse quickened.

"Nothing," he said softly, "I was just looking at your hair."

I felt my cheeks flush. *Thank God it's too dark for him to notice,* I told myself. "Oh, right, I forgot you had a thing for redheads." I tried to make my voice sound light and funny, but it came out sounding strange.

"No," he said seriously, still gazing at me, "your hair is different tonight. It looks so nice that way. . . ." His voice trailed off.

I didn't trust myself to speak. Was this just a friend complimenting me, or was this something more? And why was I desperately wishing that it *was* something more? I looked down and played with the plastic slats in the lounge chair.

"I'm sorry," he said, sounding embarrassed. "That sounded kind of lame."

"N-No, it was . . . ," I began awkwardly. "It was nice." Why was I suddenly having trouble speaking?

I didn't let myself look at him. "There are so many stars out tonight," I said in a lame attempt to change the subject and make things seem more normal. I leaned back in my chair and looked up at the sky.

"Yeah, there are," he said. "Look, there's the Big Dipper."

I shook my head. "I can never see the constellations. I think they're a big hoax," I told him.

He laughed. "Are you kidding? It's right there."

"Where?" I asked.

"Up to the left." He was pointing with his finger.

"I don't see it," I said. I really was searching the sky, but all I saw was a big jumble of stars.

Jesse got up and knelt down on the sand next to my chair. He put his head close to mine so that he could point me in the right direction. "There it is," he said slowly. I looked up to where he was looking, but all I could think about was how near he was to me. I suddenly wanted to kiss him more than anything.

"I don't think I'll ever see it," I whispered, my voice a little shaky.

At the same moment we both turned to look at the other. Suddenly our faces were centimeters apart, our eyes locked. He swept a strand of hair away from my face, and then, before I could even think about what was happening, he kissed me. And it felt so perfect, I kissed him back.

I felt goose bumps spread across my body as he put his arms around me. My head was spinning and my heart was racing, but I didn't want it to stop.

Then suddenly Jesse pulled away. "Lauren," he whispered, his expression serious.

"Yes?" I asked softly. I was so afraid he was going to tell me that we were making another mistake.

"Do you want this to happen?" His voice was husky.

"I do," I said.

And he kissed me again.

# ELEVEN

I OPENED MY eyes slowly, feeling completely disoriented. It took a few seconds for me to register that I was lying on a lounge chair, in the same clothes that I had worn the night before, and that Jesse was sleeping next to me, his head on my shoulder. We had fallen asleep at the beach.

I sat up slowly, careful not to wake him. I knew I had to get back to the Hillmans' and into my bed before anyone found out I was gone. But as I looked at Jesse's sleeping face I couldn't bear to walk away from him. Memories of the night before flooded my mind. Jesse and I had kissed for what had seemed like hours. And then we had talked . . . and cuddled . . . and kissed some more. And then we must have fallen asleep.

It had felt so right, so perfect, I couldn't fight it any longer. *Just because things don't work out for some people doesn't mean it won't work for Jesse and me,* I told myself as I watched the waves crash in on the sand.

Suddenly I realized that the sky was getting lighter, and I saw a round, fiery glow at the horizon. I turned and gently shook Jesse. "Jesse," I whispered, "Jesse, wake up."

He opened his eyes and sat up, startled. When his eyes settled on my face, he smiled. "It's you." He put a hand through my hair. "It really happened."

"Yes," I said, and pointed across the water. "Look—the sun's rising."

"Wow," he said softly. He straddled the chair, sitting behind me. As his arms wrapped around me I leaned back on his chest. "Wow," he whispered again, resting his chin on my shoulder.

It was breathtaking to watch the reddish orange ball of light make its way to the top of the sky, leaving its glow on the water and spreading light as it climbed. I had seen the sunrise before, of course, but it still sent chills through my body. And it was even more perfect to share that moment with Jesse.

When it was all over, we both sat there for a moment in each other's arms, mesmerized. "Wasn't that beautiful?" I said finally, stretching my arms over my head.

"It was." Jesse stood and pulled me up next to him. "It was so fast, though."

"I know; that's why I wanted you to catch it."

"Thank you," he said, leaning in to kiss me.

We kissed until I felt the early morning sun beat

down on my face. "We'd both better get back," I told him, reluctantly breaking away. "I'll be in serious trouble if the Hillmans find out. Besides, you've got to get some sleep before work."

He smiled. "I know, but I'd rather kiss you than sleep any day—" He started to kiss me again.

I laughed and pushed him away. "Yeah, but you may never kiss me again if I'm grounded for the rest of my life."

"Okay, then," he said, taking my hand. "Will you visit me at the pool?"

"Sure," I said. I kissed him one last time. "See you later."

I took a long look at Jesse standing by the water, and then I practically skipped to the Hillmans' house.

Hours later I woke up in my own bed. I sat up and saw that Rachel had already gotten up. Her beach bag was gone from its usual place. *She probably went to catch those peak tanning hours,* I thought.

I looked at the clock on the wall. It was already eleven-thirty. I was surprised that Rachel and Mrs. Hillman had let me sleep so late. Then I remembered that they had plans—some sort of mother-daughter tennis game with another family.

*Well, I needed that sleep after last night,* I thought as I started to get dressed. I stood by the mirror for a moment, daydreaming as I remembered

135

Jesse's smiling face, his soft kisses, his arms around my body . . .

*Chill out, Lauren,* I told myself, *you're starting to act like Rachel!*

I laughed at that thought and finished getting dressed. I headed downstairs to grab a bagel, and then I started on my way to the pool.

Tommy was the lifeguard on duty. I walked over to his chair and waved. "Hey, Tommy, how's it going?" I greeted him.

"Not bad," he answered, lifting his sunglasses away from his eyes. "How 'bout you? You seem pretty chipper today."

I smiled. "I guess I do feel good. It's a beautiful day."

"It certainly is," he agreed. "Where's Rachel?"

"I don't know. She had a tennis game this morning or something," I said, squinting at him.

"Oh, right, she told me about that yesterday. Some big game with her mother, against Jenny and Mrs. Stein."

"Right, that's it." I nodded. "Sounds thrilling. Anyway, is Jesse around?"

"Yeah, he's on a break now." He motioned over to the staff quarters. "You should try the bungalows. He was headed that way."

"Okay, thanks," I said as I started walking away. "Bye."

"Bye. Hey, I'll stop by the Hillmans' to see you guys soon," he called after me.

"Cool," I called back. I did feel bad that I hadn't

spent more time with Tommy since I'd been on the Vineyard—we had been close in the past. But Tommy seemed to want to hang out with Rachel and me together, and I wasn't quite up for that. I mean, he would expect things between Rachel and me to be the way they used to be.

*Oh, well,* I thought, *things change.* I exited the pool area and walked down the paved path toward the staff bungalows. The sets of bunkhouses subdivided into rooms were on the other side of the club, away from the more prime, beachfront locations.

The hot midday sun blazed on my skin as I walked along the path. I couldn't stop myself from smiling. I wondered if Jesse would be as excited to see me as I was to see him. I opened the gate that led to the staff housing area and laughed, realizing how happy Rachel and Kyle would be when they found out about Jesse and me.

As I rounded the corner of the first bunk unit my eyes widened in shock. Kyle stood right in the middle of the small patio, deep in a lip lock with a sundress-clad girl. A girl who was definitely not Rachel.

I covered my mouth to keep from gasping and darted back around the corner.

What was I going to do? I leaned back against the white wooden paneling, feeling dizzy. Should I confront Kyle right here, right now?

Before I had a chance to decide, I heard a familiar voice.

"How long are you staying, Alicia?"

I whipped my head around and saw that Jesse had joined Kyle and the girl. Kyle was now holding her hand in the same way he'd always held Rachel's.

"I'm not sure," she said, turning to Kyle with a big grin. "I got time off from camp, so I decided to come down and surprise Kyle."

"Isn't the camp you're working at, like, six hours away?" Jesse asked her, looking confused.

"Yeah," Alicia said, running a hand through her long, straight brown hair. "But I arranged my days off to be consecutive so that I could come here and visit. I'll be with Kyle for a week."

Jesse folded his tanned, muscular arms across his chest. "So after you leave here, you don't have another day off the entire summer?"

"What can I tell you, cuz?" Kyle said. "I have a totally devoted girlfriend."

Alicia gave Kyle a peck on his cheek. "You definitely do," she said.

I ducked back behind the building and out of sight. The scene made me sick to my stomach. A devoted girlfriend? Kyle already had a devoted girlfriend—Rachel! Finding out about Alicia would devastate her. I could have punched Kyle for deceiving her this whole time.

Obviously Kyle had known Alicia for a while—she was probably his girlfriend back home. How else would Jesse have known her?

Jesse knew her!

I swallowed hard at that thought. This explained those weird moments of tension—that first night at minigolf and then after the movie. Jesse must have been uncomfortable watching Kyle put the moves on another girl.

This whole time Jesse knew that Kyle had a girlfriend. But he hadn't said a word, either to me or to Rachel. He had been content to set Rachel up for what was sure to be a heartbreak. Images flashed in my mind: my parents, smiling and happy at their wedding; Jonathan Groff walking out of the homecoming dance with Cori; Kyle with his arm around Rachel. All broken promises and disappointments.

I was suddenly angry at myself for thinking that things would be different with Jesse. How could I have let myself care about him? Sure, the night before had been wonderful, but who knew what would happen in the future? He was bound to hurt me in the end. He was a guy, after all. He obviously didn't even think it was worth mentioning that Kyle was seeing two girls at the same time.

I had thought that Jesse was special—someone to trust. Well, trusting Jesse Shaw was a mistake I wasn't about to make twice.

Hoping to stay out of view, I took off as fast as I could.

I walked away from the club, fuming. I still couldn't believe what I had seen. I was right all along. Relationships never work. I didn't know what I'd say to Jesse. For the time being, I didn't want to see him at all.

But what would I say to Rachel? I knew I had to tell her.

I sat down on a bench by the beach, thinking as I watched people walk by. I felt so horrible for Rachel. I mean, sure, I had thought Kyle was a jerk when I first met him, but not a two-timing jerk.

And Rachel liked him so much. I had found it annoying that she went on and on about him, but she didn't deserve this. *Come to think of it,* I realized, *Rachel has the biggest heart of anyone I know.* I suddenly felt very guilty—guilty that I knew about Kyle and guilty that I hadn't made any effort to get along with her all summer.

I don't know how long I sat there before I finally stood up and walked to the beach, determined to find Rachel. I had to tell her about Kyle. Who knew how she'd take the news? From the way her face always lit up at the mere thought of him, I knew it wasn't going to be pretty. But I owed it to Rachel to let her know the truth.

I ran a hand through my thick, salty hair and scanned the beach. I knew that Rachel had to be there.

Sure enough, after searching for a couple of minutes I spotted her, stretched out on a chair in a black-and-white-checked bikini. She was wearing headphones, and her head was bobbing up and down.

I sat down on the edge of her chair. "Have you been here for a while?" I asked her.

Rachel reached to hit the stop button on her Discman and pulled the earphones out of her ears.

"Half an hour, maybe," she said. "Are you actually going to lie out?"

"I—I—felt like getting some sun," I lied. I wasn't prepared to tell her right away. "So who won the tennis game?"

"We did." She smiled proudly. Then she sat upright, looking at me with a confused look on her face. "Lauren, is something wrong?"

"No," I answered, digging my toes in the sand, "why?"

"Your forehead is doing that wrinkle thing." Her blue eyes were open wide.

Even if we hadn't been close lately, she did know me well. I took a deep breath. *Just tell her the truth.* "Look—I just saw something that I think you should know about."

"What?"

"I was at the staff bungalows, and I saw Kyle," I began slowly.

"Did he have a message for me or something?" Rachel asked excitedly.

"No, Rach," I said cautiously. I felt like I was about to drop a bomb. I had to just blurt it out. "He has a girlfriend."

"What are you talking about?" Rachel's voice was shaky. "*I'm* his girlfriend."

"He has a girlfriend from home," I told her.

"No, you must have misunderstood. There's no way that Kyle has another girlfriend," Rachel insisted.

"I saw her, Rach," I said softly. "I'm really sorry."

"No, you didn't." Rachel was shaking her head furiously. "How do you know she was his girlfriend? You can't just go jumping to ridiculous conclusions."

"I overheard him call her his girlfriend . . . and they were kissing."

Rachel didn't say anything. She just kept shaking her head. "I mean *really* kissing." I had to make her believe me.

Rachel stood up, tears in her eyes. "Why are you saying this? How can you be so mean? You've been nothing but rude to me all summer, but to lie—"

"I'm not lying—" I pleaded, standing up next to her.

"Shut up! I don't want to hear it," Rachel interrupted, a tear rolling down her cheek. "You're just bitter! You want everyone to be as lonely and unhappy as you are. Even after I made my parents invite you out here this summer . . ."

Rachel trailed off, and we stared at each other in silence. "*You* invited me here?" I asked, stunned. All along I had thought that it had been her parents' idea.

"Yeah, well, what difference does it make?" she snapped, brushing the tears from her eyes. I had never seen her so upset. "You don't want to be here. That's fine. You don't want to have anything to do with me. That's fine too. But why do you have to try to turn me against Kyle? Why can't you just let us be happy?"

Before I could say a word, she stormed off the beach.

*Rachel* had asked her parents to invite me to Martha's Vineyard for the summer? I had assumed all along that her parents had forced her into it just like I had been forced. Suddenly it made sense why we were sharing a room.

I closed my eyes and tilted my face toward the sun, letting out a sigh. I had been wrong about everything lately—I was wrong about Rachel, wrong about Jesse. Rachel was the person I should have trusted, not Jesse. And she was right. I had been nothing but rude to her the whole summer.

I decided that I would go for a walk and give her some time to cool off before I tried to talk to her again. She had been really angry, but I knew that she would realize the truth sooner or later—especially since Kyle's girlfriend was in town for a few days.

I would be there for Rachel when she needed me. I stood up, wiping the sand off my legs. I was determined to make it up to Rachel.

And I was determined never to talk to Jesse Shaw again.

# TWELVE

I CAME BACK to the Hillmans' house a couple of hours later. The walk had helped me to clear my head, and I hoped that Rachel would at least talk to me.

I ran up the stairs, vowing to myself to patch things up with Rachel if it was humanly possible. I opened the door to our bedroom slowly, preparing my words for a profuse apology.

Rachel was sitting on her bed, knees up, hugging a pillow. Her eyes were red and swollen, and her normally perfect complexion was all blotchy. She was surrounded by balled-up tissues.

"Rach, I'm so—"

She shook her head and put a hand out to silence me. "No, Lauren," she said, still sniffling, "I'm sorry. I'm sorry I said those horrible things to you. I should've believed you in the first place."

"No, you were right. I have been a jerk lately," I said softly.

"I should've been more understanding, what with your parents' divorce—" Rachel started to say.

"You've been nothing but understanding," I interrupted. I already felt guilty enough without listening to Rachel blame herself.

I walked into the adjoining bathroom to get another box of tissues and handed it to her. "It was really your idea to invite me here out here this summer?" I asked timidly.

She took the tissues and looked down at her pillow. She nodded silently.

"I didn't know you even cared about my parents' divorce," I said. "You never said anything to me about it."

Rachel looked up at me. "I never said anything because I didn't think you'd want to hear it from me. We haven't exactly been that close lately," she explained. "But when I heard about your parents, I felt horrible. I've always been so close to them that it was if my own parents were getting divorced. And then I figured that if I was upset, you must've felt thirty times worse."

I reached over to hug her. "You're such a good friend," I said, "much better than I deserve." As I hugged her I noticed that the pink stuffed animal Kyle had given her was crammed into the trash can in the corner of the room.

"Can I ask you something?" I said as I pulled away.

She nodded.

"What made you realize that I was telling you the truth about Kyle?"

"Oh, God, he's such a jerk." Tears began to well up in her eyes again as she spoke. She took a deep breath before she continued. "I called him because we were supposed to have dinner tonight. And then he told me that his best friend from home came to visit him, so he'd have to cancel plans with me."

I shook my head in disgust. "What a snake."

Rachel's voice was getting shakier. "I guess I knew deep down that you wouldn't lie to me, but I just didn't want to believe it was true." She paused for a moment to blow her nose. "So then I asked him why I couldn't go to dinner with him and his friend. I mean, I would think that he would want his friend to meet me."

"So what did he say?"

"He gave me some big ridiculous excuse that didn't make any sense. So I confronted him. I told him that I knew he had a girlfriend." Rachel started to cry, tears rolling down her cheeks. "And you know what, the jerk couldn't even deny it. I had caught him so off guard that he didn't know what to say."

"I can't believe that," I said softly. I walked into the bathroom to get Rachel a glass of water. "What did you do?" I asked, handing her the glass.

Rachel took a sip of water and shook her head. "I don't even know. I was so angry, I just started yelling, telling him how much I hated him, that I never wanted to talk to him again. He tried to apologize, but I didn't let him. Eventually I just hung up on him."

"Good for you," I said soothingly.

"Not really," she mumbled. "I wish I had gotten him back in some way. I just feel like such a fool."

"Rachel, you're not a fool," I told her.

"Yes, I am," she said, tears welling up again. "You know how much I liked Kyle. I really fell for that slime."

"How could you have known?" I said, trying to make her feel better. "You had no idea what he was really like."

"I could have listened to you," she choked out. "You tried to warn me. All I did was call you a liar."

"Forget about that," I said. "I already have. You can't blame yourself for this anymore, Rach. Kyle's the one who should feel bad, not you."

"I know." She sighed. "But I doubt he's spent any time crying over me. He's probably with his girlfriend right now, kissing her like he kissed me." She focused on the pink stuffed animal in the garbage can for a couple of moments. I could tell that she was trying to keep herself from crying again. "Oh, no," she said suddenly.

"What?" I asked.

"Next week's the annual Club Day," she said. "Kyle and I were supposed to go together."

I had forgotten all about Club Day. It was an event that the club did every year—there was a barbecue on the beach by the club, and they closed off all the decks, setting up booths and games. The fair went on all afternoon, and the following evening there was the midsummer dinner dance at the club.

All the proceeds went to charity. "Who needs Kyle?" I said to Rachel. "We always had a great time at Club Day in the past—just the two of us—without guys."

Rachel stood up. "You know what, you're right." She straightened up her pillows and gathered her crumpled-up tissues. "Who needs guys?"

"That's the attitude," I said encouragingly.

"You were right to only want to be friends with Jesse," she went on. "Guys *are* nothing but trouble."

The mention of Jesse caught me off guard. I sat on the edge of the bed and didn't say anything for a moment. I had been so worried about Rachel that I had forgotten how mad I was at Jesse.

Rachel didn't even notice that I was in my own world. She was walking around the room, straightening up and mumbling about how worthless guys were. I didn't hear everything she said because images of my night with Jesse were filling my head.

"So what do you say?" Rachel sat down next to me. "Are you ready to have a great summer with just us girls, no guys involved?"

Rachel was staring at me, waiting for a response. For a split second I hesitated, thinking of how much fun I'd had with Jesse. But then I reminded myself of what a slime Kyle was—and that Jesse was a liar. I smiled at Rachel. "It sounds good to me," I said.

"Cool." Rachel hugged me. "You know, one good thing did come out of this whole Kyle mess."

"What's that?"

"I finally feel like we're really friends again," she said.

"Yeah, that's true," I agreed. "I'm really glad."

"Hey, I have an idea," Rachel said. "Let's go get chocolate fudge squares at Hilliard's!"

When we were little, going to Hilliard's Kitch-in-vue for fudge was one of our favorite activities. The old-fashioned candy shop was in a cottage that could have been straight out of Hansel and Gretel. I hadn't been there in years. "Great idea," I told her.

We jumped off the bed and headed out to our bikes, ready to continue our summer—guy-free.

A couple of hours later Rachel and I returned to the house, feeling slightly nauseous from the chocolate overload. But it had been delicious and fun. Except for a few tearful moments I was able to keep Rachel's mind off Kyle. And since I was putting so much effort into cheering up Rachel, I hadn't thought about Jesse. We'd stopped at the video store to pick up a couple of movies, both of us in the mood to spend the evening snuggled up next to the TV.

"Oh, here she is—perfect timing. Hold on a moment," Mrs. Hillman said into the phone as we walked through the door. She put her hand over the receiver and whispered to me, "Lauren, honey, phone's for you. I think it's that boy, Jesse."

I realized that Jesse didn't know I was angry with him. He probably wondered why I had never shown up at the pool that day. *Well,* I thought, *it shouldn't take me long to let him know what a jerk he is.* "Thanks," I said, "I'll take it upstairs."

Rachel was looking at me questioningly. I hadn't told her that Jesse and I had kissed, and I figured that I never would. I just wanted to forget about it. As far as she knew, Jesse and I were just friends. "I'll only be a minute," I said to her as I headed upstairs. "You get the movie ready."

I walked up the stairs, gathering my thoughts. *I'll just tell him what happened and then I'll hang up,* I told myself.

I grabbed the phone and sank down into my bed. "Hello?"

"Lauren, hi—where have you been?" Jesse sounded confused.

"I've been hanging out with Rach, trying to heal her broken heart," I said coolly.

"Oh, yeah, Kyle told me about their fight," Jesse said. "I figured she was probably upset. But I was wondering why you didn't come by to see me, or call me, or—"

"I did come by," I cut in sharply. "And I saw you and Kyle and *Alicia.* I can't believe that you knew all along Kyle had a girlfriend and you didn't tell me!"

Silence. "So that's what this is about," Jesse said, sighing audibly. "Listen, I knew it was wrong not to tell you, but I didn't think that you'd really care. I mean, we were always saying how Rachel and Kyle were so annoying, how they deserved each other. . . ."

"And you thought that meant Rachel deserved to be lied to?" I said to Jesse in disbelief.

"No, it's just—just . . . when did you start caring so much about Rachel anyway?" Jesse stammered. "I thought you didn't even like her, Lauren."

"Since I realized that Rachel was a true friend," I answered hotly. "Unlike you, Rachel would never lie, Jesse."

"Look," Jesse said slowly, "I should have told you what was going on. But you can't hold this against me forever. This can't mean that things are over between us."

I took a deep breath. "Actually, Jesse, that *is* what this means. You've given me even more reason to believe that relationships can't work and guys can't be trusted." And with that I hung up the phone.

I paced around the room for a moment to calm myself down before going back downstairs. I felt tears starting to form in my eyes, but I held them back.

He wasn't worth it. No guy was. I walked into the bathroom, splashed some cold water on my face, and headed out of the room, ready to spend the evening watching movies with an old friend.

# THIRTEEN

"I FORGOT HOW much fun this day is," Rachel said to me a week later as we waited in line to get our tickets for Club Day. In order to play any of the games at the booths or buy any food, you had to pay with tickets.

It was a gorgeous sunny day, and the club and the nearby beach was packed with families, children, teenagers, and older people. The decks were lined with colorful booths, and there was a moon bounce and a small Ferris wheel at the far end. A college band played reggae music on a stage on the beach, and the smell of the barbecue mixed with the smells of cotton candy, caramel apples, and sunscreen wafted through the afternoon air. Everyone seemed to be in a great mood.

Even Rachel. I was really proud of the way she was handling the whole Kyle situation. Once again I reminded myself that I hadn't given her enough credit.

Sure, she'd had a few breakdowns during the week, but I was always able to cheer her up. I watched her as she took in all the sights of the boardwalk. She looked beautiful—you would never have known that she was the recent victim of a heartbreak. Her blond hair was pulled back into a ponytail, and her blue eyes were shining.

"So what do you want to do first?" I asked her after we each had purchased a roll of tickets.

"I guess we're too old for the Moon Bounce." Rachel giggled, peering at the kids jumping around inside the huge orange structure. "Should we go down to the beach?"

"Sure." I nodded. The beach barbecue was where everyone our age hung out.

When we got there, we saw that there was plenty of dancing already going on and hordes of people were crowded around the barbecue, waiting to get their hands on a hamburger or a grilled chicken sandwich. Rachel and I each grabbed a Coke from the ice-filled garbage cans and found a spot off to the side to sit down.

We weren't really talking, just people watching and taking in the scene, slowly sipping our drinks. "Hey, there's Jesse," Rachel said, gesturing over to the food area.

I glanced over, and sure enough, there he was, sitting on a blanket with Roni. She was talking to him animatedly. I winced as I saw her playfully poke him in the stomach. He didn't seem to be say-ing much. *It figures that he already found somebody else,* I thought. *I guess Jesse doesn't find her pushy anymore.*

I had to fight back the jealous rage brewing inside me. Then I remembered that Rachel didn't know about anything that had happened between me and Jesse. I wanted to keep it that way. "Yeah, I see him," I said nonchalantly.

"Oh, God," she said suddenly, "I hope I don't see Kyle. I don't think I'm ready for that yet." She had a stricken look on her face.

"Don't even think about it," I said.

"You're right—I've got to keep him out of my mind." She stood up. "I'm going to get something to eat; you want anything?"

"Nah, I'll wait here."

"Okay." She walked to the barbecue and got in line behind a couple of guys in fraternity T-shirts.

Jesse was now standing to the right of the barbecue, eating a hamburger. Roni was still with him, but he didn't seem to be talking to her. I looked at him for a moment, wondering how I could have fallen for him. Unfortunately I let my eyes stay for a second too long because he caught me looking.

I quickly darted my eyes away and pretended that I hadn't seen him. When I looked back at Rachel, who was getting her chicken off the grill, I saw something much worse. Rachel was completely oblivious to the fact that Kyle and Alicia were standing a few people behind her in line. And they weren't just standing; they were cuddling and kissing and acting like a couple. I immediately got up and started walking over to Rachel. I had to distract her. I couldn't let her see them. . . .

But as I was walking, I realized that Jesse had noticed Kyle and Alicia too. He started walking toward Rachel from the other direction. He got to her before I did and put his arm around her shoulders, directing her away from Kyle.

They were coming toward me, Jesse's arm still around Rachel's shoulders. Rachel was holding her chicken sandwich in one hand, looking slightly confused. "I was just telling Rachel here how you and I made a bet on whether I could win the biggest stuffed animal at the club today," Jesse said. "I'm ready to show you guys my stuff."

I knew he was just trying to distract Rachel, but he was a pretty good liar. *Unfortunately I already know he has no trouble lying,* I thought. At that moment I had to forget about how angry I was at Jesse. I had to look out for Rachel and keep her from seeing Kyle.

"Okay," I said, looking at Rachel and barely acknowledging Jesse. "C'mon, Rach, let's go. I have money riding on this," I told her.

She furrowed her brow. "Okay, I guess," she said. "Let me just get a napkin for my sandwich."

Before we could stop her, Rachel was walking back to the food area. *Oh, no,* I thought, *she's going to see them.* But by some sort of stroke of luck Kyle and Alicia had left the food line. I searched for them and saw them walking toward the main deck. "There they are," I whispered to Jesse, pointing them out.

"Uh–oh," Jesse said, "I guess we can't go to the—" Before he could finish his sentence, Rachel was back, napkin and sandwich in hand.

"Okay, let's see what you can win." She smiled.

Jesse and I stood there for a second, not moving and not saying anything. I looked around, trying to think of an excuse not to go to the games.

The band was no longer on the stage. Now it was a deejay—a dorky-looking guy in his thirties. He had just started to play the "club song," this cheesy pop song that had become the Beach Club's anthem.

"C'mon, everybody," the deejay called out, "where's your club spirit? Let's all do the club dance!"

"The club dance!" Jesse repeated. "I love the club dance!" He took Rachel's free hand in his. "Rach, will you come dance with me?"

Now Rachel looked really confused. "But I thought you wanted to go play some games—" she started.

"But they're playing the club song now," he insisted. "Let's go!"

"Why don't you dance with Lauren?" she asked. "I'll eat my sandwich."

"No, Rach." I shook my head. "You know that I can't stand these cheesy songs."

She giggled. "That's true. I can't really imagine you out there." Then she paused a moment and looked at Jesse with a bewildered expression on her face. "But I didn't think that *you'd* want to dance to this either, Jesse. It doesn't seem like your type of thing."

Jesse smiled. "What can I say? I'm full of surprises." He tugged on her hand, pulling her toward the dance area. "Come on!"

"Okay, okay, already." Rachel laughed. She handed me her sandwich, and they ran off to dance.

I watched them as they became part of the crowd moving to the beat of the music. They started to do the hand and body movements that went along with the song, following the deejay's instructions.

I laughed to myself. That was a good save by Jesse. I knew that he didn't really like to dance, especially the dorky club dance. I smiled as I watched him pretend to enjoy himself—I knew it was the last thing that he wanted to do. *Serves him right,* I thought.

And most important, Rachel looked as though she was really having fun. She loved to dance. She was smiling brightly, and she looked relaxed and carefree.

They kept dancing after the club song was over. I watched as he twirled her around with exaggerated dance moves. It was nice of Jesse to give her so much attention. But if he had told her about Kyle in the first place, this whole mess would have never even happened.

I sat down on a nearby lounge chair and continued to watch them. I took a bite of Rachel's sandwich, figuring that she probably didn't want it any longer.

Suddenly Tommy walked up from behind and sat down next to me. "Hey, Laur," he said.

"Hey, what's up?" I gave him a smile.

"Not much," he said, "just doing the barbecue thing, you know."

"Yup." I looked back at Rachel and Jesse, who were still dancing.

Tommy followed my line of vision. "Oh, *there's* Rach," he said. He watched her for a moment. "It's good to see her happy."

I looked at him questioningly.

"I heard about Kyle," he explained. "It's all around the club what a jerk he is."

"He's scum," I said.

"Yeah. I could kill him for hurting Rachel." He shook his head. "But she does seem to be doing okay."

"She's strong." Rachel and Jesse had stopped dancing and were walking toward us. "Hey, Tommy—" I started.

"Yeah?" he responded.

"Do you think you could watch out for Rachel for the rest of the day? I have a headache. I think I'm going to head back to the Hillmans'." That was partly true. My head was starting to pound. But it was more that I didn't feel like talking to Jesse. I knew that I didn't want to be with him, and spending time with him would only confuse me.

"No problem," Tommy said as Rachel and Jesse

came up to us.

"Hey, guys," Rachel called to us, still looking happy.

"You looked good out there," Tommy told her.

"Thanks." She blushed. "Who would've known that Jesse was a good dancer?"

Jesse shrugged. "I try to keep it a secret." His face was slightly flushed. He ran his fingers through his hair and gave me a tiny smile.

I stood up abruptly. "Rach, I'm going to go home. I've got a bad headache." I made a point not to look at Jesse again.

"Are you okay?" She sounded concerned. "Do you want me to come?"

"No, no," I assured her. "I just need to get some rest. I'll be fine." I kissed her on the cheek. "Hang out with Tommy. I'll see you later."

I started to walk away.

"Bye, feel better!" Rachel called.

Jesse started to walk with me. "Lauren, can we please talk?" he asked when we were out of Rachel's earshot.

I stopped walking and looked at him, shaking my head. "Listen, I think that it was cool of you to distract Rachel and all, but I still don't want to talk to you." I looked away from his pleading brown eyes and added quietly, "Please just leave me alone."

As I neared the Hillmans' house I longed to get into bed and go to sleep. I didn't want to think about anything—or anyone—at all. Jesse had me so confused. After I'd found out about Kyle, I had been so sure that I didn't want to have anything to do with him anymore. But that had been really sweet of him to dance with Rachel like that . . . maybe I had been too hard on him. . . .

But then I opened the front door and reality slapped me in the face: My parents were sitting on the couch in the living room. They didn't notice me walk in, and I could tell from their disgruntled expressions that they were in the middle of an argument.

"Mom? Dad?" I said, completely shocked to see them there.

"Sweetie!" My mother jumped up to give me a hug.

"Hi, pumpkin." My dad stood up and kissed my cheek.

I took a step back from them, bewildered. "What are you guys doing here?"

"We came to surprise you," my mother said. "We figured we'd come for the Midsummer Ball."

"We were about to go to the Beach Club to find you," my dad said. "We're just waiting for Marilyn and Jerry to get ready. Why aren't you at Club Day?"

"I was," I said quietly, "but I had a headache, so I came home." A surprise visit from my parents was the last thing that I needed. "You guys came together?" I asked them. They had so much trouble getting along, I couldn't understand why they'd come visit me at the same time.

"We didn't plan on it," my dad explained, "but we unknowingly both took the same days off from work." I noticed that he shot my mother an annoyed look after he said this.

"And your father was inflexible as always," my mom said angrily. "He wouldn't change his vacation days."

"I couldn't just rearrange my whole schedule, Carol," my father snapped. "You could've come at a different time too."

"Don't go blaming me," my mom argued back. "I told your secretary weeks ago that this was when I was going to visit Lauren. If you had only listened . . ."

I collapsed in a love seat as my parents continued to fight, letting out a big sigh. *This is why you can't forgive Jesse,* I reminded myself, *because all relationships end up this way—a total mess.*

I sat there for a couple of minutes, trying to tune my parents out. I couldn't believe that they hadn't even asked me about my summer yet. I felt anger boiling up inside me as my parents' voices got louder and louder. Luckily Mr. and Mrs. Hillman came down the stairs, saving me.

When my parents saw them enter the room, they both stopped arguing and smiled at them, pretending as if nothing was wrong.

"Lauren," Mrs. Hillman said, "you're back. We were just going to look for you and Rachel."

"Rachel's still there," I said. "I had enough of

Club Day."

"I guess if you've seen one Club Day, you've seen them all," my father joked.

"We'll stay here so that we can talk to Lauren," my mother told the Hillmans. "You go on to the boardwalk without us."

"No," I said a little too suddenly, causing all four adults to stare at me questioningly. "I mean, my head is really pounding. I need to get some sleep." My parents looked disappointed. I felt a little guilty, but I really couldn't handle being alone with them that afternoon. "Why don't you guys go and enjoy yourself? We'll hang out tonight and tomorrow."

Nobody said anything for a moment. Then my mom broke the silence. "Okay, sweetie, if you really aren't feeling well—"

"You'll have plenty of time to spend together," Mrs. Hillman whispered to my mom. "Everyone needs some resting time."

"All right," my father agreed, bending over to kiss me, "but we have a lot of catching up to do when we get back."

"Sure." I nodded.

"Bye, hon." My mom kissed me too.

"We'll see you later, Lauren," Mr. Hillman said. The four of them got themselves organized, said "good-bye" and "feel better" about a hundred times, and then were finally out the door.

I remained sitting in the love seat the whole time, hugging my knees. After they left, I breathed deeply, relieved that there was silence. I dropped my head down into my knees and closed my eyes. A lump was rising in my throat, and tears were forming in my eyes.

Suddenly I heard the front door open and the sound of footsteps in the hallway. *They can't be back already,* I thought. *I hope they didn't change their minds and decide to stay here with me.*

But then a voice called out, "Hello? Anybody home?"

I knew that voice—it was Jesse's.

I sat up straight, letting go of my knees, and tried to wipe my eyes dry with my hands. *I could hide and pretend I'm not here,* I thought. I still didn't want to see Jesse—what was the point? But before I had a chance to do anything, he walked into the living room and saw me sitting there.

"Lauren," he said as he came over and sat down next to me, "the door was open, so I just let myself in."

I nodded silently and looked down at my hands.

He let out a big sigh. "Listen, I know you said you didn't want to talk to me, but I had to come and—" He paused midsentence. "Lauren, do you think you can at least look at me?"

I obliged, still not saying a word. I hated to look at those amazing eyes of his, the eyes that had attracted me to him in the first place.

"God, Laur, are you okay?" he asked. I must not have done a very good job of drying my tears.

"Not really," I said bitterly. "My parents came to give me a surprise visit."

"Where are they?" He looked around the room.

"I sent them to the club." I pulled out the elastic that was holding my hair back, letting my thick hair fall over my face. "I was with them for all of ten minutes, and they were arguing for about nine and a half of them," I said glumly, playing with the elastic.

"I'm sorry," Jesse said softly, brushing some strands of hair off my face. "That's really hard."

"Yeah," I said, "it is. So I would appreciate it if you would just let me be. My parents are living proof that falling in love is a very bad idea."

"Lauren, I understand why you're upset with your parents, but don't shut *me* out because of it," he pleaded.

I didn't say anything.

"I mean, can't we at least be friends? You at least owe me that."

I stood up and looked down at him, narrowing my eyes. "I don't owe you anything. *You* lied to *me*, remember?" I started to walk out of the room and toward the stairs.

Jesse followed me. "So that's it, huh?" His voice was angry. "You're never going to go out with anybody your whole life?"

I ran up the stairs and turned around when I got to the top. Jesse was standing at the bottom, looking up at me, with his arms folded across his chest. I couldn't hide the tears that were falling down my cheeks. "Yeah, that's it," I said in a shaky voice. And then I walked away, leaving Jesse standing there alone.

# FOURTEEN

"YOUR PARENTS SEEM to be getting along okay," Rachel said to me the following evening as we were getting dressed for the dinner dance at the club.

I snorted. "They've been on their very best behavior in front of you and your parents. But the minute I'm alone with the two of them, the war starts again."

It was true that they'd pretty much refrained from fighting the past day and a half. But that was partly due to my careful efforts in keeping them apart. I had spent the morning with my dad and Mr. Hillman and the afternoon with my mom, Rachel, and Mrs. Hillman. We had eaten every meal with both families together, but I had made sure that my parents always sat at opposite ends of the table.

But I was dreading the dinner dance. We would be seated by families, and my parents would have to sit together. Plus, I knew that all the other parents would get up to dance and mingle at some point, leaving my parents alone to argue.

"Maybe they're starting to work things out," Rachel said optimistically.

"Maybe," I answered, with a doubtful tone to my voice.

"So," Rachel said, twirling around in front of me, "do you like this dress?" She was wearing a short white dress with spaghetti straps and pale pink flowers. Her thick blond hair fell across her shoulders, and the dress really showed off her tan.

"Yeah, I love it," I told her. "You look really great."

"Thanks." She smiled brightly. I watched her move around the room as she continued to get ready, putting on her shoes and looking for the right earrings to wear.

"Rach, I'm really proud of you," I said, not caring how corny it sounded. "You're handling this Kyle thing so well."

"Um, thanks," she responded. She walked over to her makeup drawer and began furiously to look for something.

I was suspicious. Rachel only fidgeted like that when she was holding something back. "Rach? What exactly are you looking for?"

"Huh?" she answered, still rifling through the drawer. "Oh, um, nothing; just this . . . this . . . uh . . . lipstick." She pulled out an ancient-looking lipstick to show me. It was a bright pink color that I'd never seen her wear—and it was so ugly that I hoped she never did.

I put my hands on my hips. "Is there something you're not telling me?"

She looked down at the plush white carpet. "Well, um—" she started.

"Rach," I said, suddenly worried, "you didn't forgive Kyle, did you?"

"God, no!" She opened her eyes wide, showing her shock. "No, I would never forgive that slime! I can't believe that you think I would!"

"I *didn't* think you would," I told her, "but you're bopping around the room, fidgeting like crazy—it's obvious that something's going on. And I'm trying to think of something that you wouldn't want to tell me—"

Rachel laughed. "I can't hide anything from you."

"Hide what?" I asked impatiently. I was so curious.

She pulled me over to her bed so we could sit down while she told me. "Remember how you left me with Tommy when you went home yesterday?" she started excitedly.

"Yeah."

"Well, I mean, I never looked at Tommy as anything but a friend before. He's little Tommy, you know? I just never thought of him in *that* way—but then yesterday he looked so cute, and he was so sweet and—"

"Wait a minute," I interrupted, not believing what I was hearing, "are you telling me that you and Tommy—"

"Yes!" She jumped off the bed as if she couldn't

contain herself any longer. "We kissed! And I *really* like him!"

"Whoa, whoa," I said, trying to process this information, "back up. How did this happen?"

Rachel took a deep breath and sat back down. "Okay," she began, "here's what happened. Tommy would always come visit me on the beach. You know, before you and I worked things out, I spent a lot of time by myself, lying out in the sun."

"Right," I said, "go on."

"Kyle usually worked the day shift, so I wouldn't even see him. So Tommy would come by on his break, and we'd talk or play cards—sometimes he'd bring me a snack or a drink or something."

"That was nice of him," I said, encouraging her to go on.

"Yeah, it was. But like I said, I never looked at him that way. I wasted all my time thinking about Kyle." She pretended to gag. "But I felt totally comfortable around Tommy. We became closer friends. And then yesterday he was so sweet to me. We spent the afternoon together—we danced, we went on the Ferris wheel, walked around the dock. I started to look at him differently. I noticed that he *is* really good-looking. And then before I knew it, he was telling me that he had liked me for a really long time, like, since last summer!"

She paused to give me a minute to process all of this.

"Wow," I said.

"I know." She nodded. "I couldn't believe it either. But then it seemed so natural and right, and I realized that I liked him too. And then we kissed." She collapsed back on the bed with a dreamy expression on her face. "And it was wonderful." She sighed. Then she sat up suddenly and looked at me, beaming. "So whaddya think?"

I hugged her. "I'm so happy for you," I said, smiling back.

"Really?"

"Of course," I told her, "you deserve this. Tommy is a totally great guy."

"I was afraid to tell you," Rachel admitted, looking a little embarrassed. "I mean—after we made that pact about a guy-free summer and all."

The image of Jesse standing at the bottom of the Hillmans' stairs flashed in my mind. I quickly chased it away. "Don't be ridiculous. I just want you to be happy—if Tommy makes you happy—"

"He does," she said, grinning.

"Well, I'm glad." I paused for a minute, thinking about everything she had just told me. "I do have to admit," I continued, "I'm kind of surprised that you would want to go out with someone right now. I mean, that you would trust a guy after Kyle and everything."

"Kyle did hurt me. But Tommy's not Kyle. It's a totally different situation," she said.

"You said that stuff about guys being nothing but trouble and all," I reminded her.

"Well, yeah," she acknowledged. She stood up and started to put on her makeup in front of the mirror. "But I was just really angry and totally hurt. I don't really think that *all* guys are trouble."

"Right," I said softly. I got my dress out of the closet and started to get ready. I really was happy for Rachel, but I couldn't believe that she could still be so optimistic about relationships after Kyle had turned out to be such a snake. *But then again,* I thought, *she and Tommy really do make a good couple—she should go out with him.*

"I'm totally psyched for tonight," she said, spraying some perfume on her wrists. "I haven't really seen Tommy today—what with your parents visiting and all—so tonight should be really fun."

"I'm sure you'll have a great time with him," I assured her, thinking of the miserable night with my parents that lay ahead of me. "Will you zip me?" I asked her.

"Sure," she said, moving over. "It's too bad Jesse isn't coming—he's such a good dancer." She patted me on the back. "You're all zipped."

I turned around to face her, caught off guard by Jesse's name. "How do you know he's not coming?"

"Oh, I bumped into him. He told me he wasn't going to make it." She stepped back, looking at me. "Hey, that dress looks amazing on you."

I turned to look at myself in the mirror. I did love the dress. It was just a simple short black dress, but it fit my body well. "Thanks," I said a little distractedly. Because at that moment all I was thinking about was Jesse.

*It's better if he's not at the dance,* I told myself. *Rachel might be ready to trust someone again, but I'm not.*

★　　★　　★

The tone for the evening was set when Mr. Hillman suggested that we take two cars over to the dinner dance—the Tylers in one car and the Hillmans in the other. I'm sure it seemed logical to him, but I knew that putting my parents in a car together was a bad idea.

My parents agreed to this plan through obviously gritted teeth, so Mrs. Hillman made another suggestion: The females would go in one car, the males in the other. Then my parents were embarrassed. They didn't want it to seem like they were so petty that they couldn't ride in a car together for less than two miles, even though that was the truth. So they insisted that we go back to the first plan—Hillmans in one car, Tylers in the other.

The last thing on earth that I wanted to do was ride in a car alone with my parents, so I made Rachel come along with us. Of course, during the ten minutes it took us to drive over to the club and find a parking space, less than five words were spoken.

By the time we got to the dinner dance, it had already been a long night. Because of our lengthy discussion over who would ride in what car, we were late. When we walked into the ballroom, everyone else was already seated. A waiter led us to the Hillmans' reserved table at the edge of the dance floor. It was set for six, and small dinner salads had been placed at the seats.

I sat down with my parents on one side of me and Rachel on the other. Rachel was actively scanning the room. She leaned her head in to me and whispered, "Tommy must be eating in the staff room." There was a separate, smaller dining room where the staff ate. They could come in and dance after the dinner was served. "I hope he comes to find me later," she said anxiously.

"I'm sure he will," I told her.

"Yeah, me too."

A waiter came by and told us the dinner selections for the evening. I ordered the pasta primavera. The club had done a good job of preparing for the dance. The ballroom was elegantly decorated with flowing white streamers. Tall white candles and large flower arrangements were at the center of every table. There was a jazz band playing on the dance floor, and the room was filled with the sounds of music and laughter.

For most of the dinner my parents got along. They were mostly gossiping with the Hillmans about different members of the club. I found their conversation boring, so I pretty much tuned them out and just talked to Rachel. *As long as they're not fighting, I don't care what they talk about,* I thought as I picked at my pasta.

The trouble started when the coffee and dessert arrived. That's when the band struck up and people began to rise from their tables. "Excuse us," Mrs. Hillman said as she and Mr. Hillman stood, "this is our song." They walked to the dance floor, holding hands. *Why can't my parents be like that?* I wondered for the millionth time.

Then a second later Tommy walked over to the

table. He sat down in Mrs. Hillman's empty seat, on the other side of Rachel, and kissed her on the cheek. "Hey, Rachel; hey, Laur."

"Hi, Tommy," I said. He and Rachel were beaming at each other. I turned to my parents and said, "Mom, Dad? You remember Tommy, don't you?"

"Of course," my mom said. "It's been a long time since we've seen you. You guys are all getting so tall!"

"How are you doing, Tommy?" my father asked.

"Great, thanks," Tommy answered. I had never seen him look so happy—I could tell that he *really* liked Rachel.

"How are your parents?" my mother asked.

"They're good. They didn't rent a house out here this summer, so I'm living in the staff bungalows," he explained.

"Well, tell them we say hi," my mom said.

"Sure thing." Tommy smiled at my parents. Then he looked back at Rachel, who was gazing at him. "You wanna go dance, Rach?"

"I'd love to."

"Good seeing you, Mr. and Mrs. Tyler," Tommy called as the two of them walked away from us.

"Such a nice boy," my mom said.

"Are they a couple now?" my father asked me.

"Sort of." I started to play with the sugar cubes that were sitting in front of me in a white porcelain dish. I was glad that Rachel and Tommy found each other, but I was not pleased to be left alone with my parents.

We all sat there in an awkward silence for what

seemed like hours, watching the scene around us. The staff was setting up what looked to be a great dessert buffet. On it were mini-napoleons, eclairs, and iced brownies. Next to the rich-looking chocolate mousse there was a huge cake that said "A Midsummer Night's Ball" in gold letters. And on the far end they were putting out the trimmings for a make-your-own-sundae stand.

I was planning which desserts to attack first when I noticed a familiar face. Kyle was straightening out the spoons. Alicia must have gone back to camp. *Serves him right to have to work tonight,* I thought, noting how geeky he looked in his formal waiter's uniform. *All the more difficult for him to prey on other unsuspecting victims.*

"I don't know why you couldn't come a different week," my father muttered to my mother, finally breaking the silence. "We should've visited Lauren separately."

"I don't think we need to discuss this in front of Lauren," my mom snapped back. "If you didn't always insist on making a scene, this would be a lot easier."

"Making a scene?" My dad let out a little laugh. "I wouldn't dream of making a scene, Carol. That's *your* strong suit."

I rolled my eyes. They couldn't even be civil to each other for my sake. "It's really good to see you guys," I mumbled sarcastically.

"What does that mean?" my mom asked.

"It means that I knew this would happen the second I saw you guys sitting in the Hillmans' living

174

room," I answered, taking a sip of water.

"Lauren," my mother began, "that's not really fair. Your father and I are trying very hard to—"

"No, you're not," I interrupted. "How can you say that after the stupid fight you two just picked?"

For a moment nobody said anything. "I wish you two would grow up," I said finally.

"Lauren," my dad began, "I don't think—"

"It's just a difficult time now, honey." My mother cut him off. "But when you're older, you'll understand."

"Carol," my father snapped, turning to my mother, "I was speaking and you interrupted. *I* was talking to Lauren. You seem to forget that she's my daughter too."

"You are such a control freak!" my mom spat back. "You just can't handle it when something doesn't go your way."

If I wasn't furious with my parents, I probably would have laughed. The two of them would fight about anything under the sun. I decided that the best thing I could do at that moment was to try and tune them out.

*Rachel, where are you when I really need you?* I wondered silently.

I scanned the dance floor, hoping to find her and Tommy so I could send them some kind of a distress signal. But I couldn't spot them in the crowd. Just when I thought I was really going to lose it, somebody tapped my shoulder.

When I turned my head, I saw that it was Jesse,

hovering above me. I had to swallow hard to keep my breathing steady.

"Jesse," I said. "Um, hi."

"Hi." He leaned over so that his head was at my level. "Do you want to dance?"

Despite my promise to keep away from Jesse, there was no way that I could refuse his offer. It was my ticket away from my parents.

"Sure." I rose from my seat.

My parents paused from their fighting long enough to notice that I was heading out to the dance floor. I was sure that they were looking Jesse over as he led me to an opening in the crowd.

The song that the band was playing happened to be a slow one. Jesse put his arms around my waist, and I wrapped mine behind his head, resting my cheek on his shoulder. I was so relieved to be away from my parents' arguing, I almost felt like crying.

"So those are your parents," Jesse said to me.

"Unfortunately, yes," I answered. I paused. "Thanks, Jesse, you really came at the right moment." I couldn't keep my voice from trembling.

I felt Jesse's arms tighten around me.

I tried to ignore the fact that my heart was beating faster. "Rachel told me that you weren't going to come tonight."

"I wasn't going to." He let out a sigh. "After you told me to leave you alone yesterday, I didn't exactly feel like seeing you here. I knew that you'd look amazing—and you do."

I blushed, and my pulse raced. I didn't know

what to say—I wasn't sure what I felt.

"And I knew that it would drive me crazy to see you and not be able to talk to you," he continued.

"So why did you come?" I asked softly.

"Because I knew that your parents were visiting, and from what you'd said yesterday, I thought you might need some help," he explained.

"That was so thoughtful of you," I said, my voice choked.

He tilted his head toward mine. "What can I say? I guess I've always wanted to be a knight in shining armor."

"I think you were born a few centuries too late for that," I murmured.

"Maybe not," he replied. "After all, I am a life-guard. I get paid to rescue people."

For a moment we danced without saying a word, and my mind flashed back to the dream I'd had about Jesse. The one where I dove into the water to flee from my parents, and Jesse had taught me to swim.

I remembered the way I felt in the dream that night, warm and safe. It was just the way I was feeling now as Jesse held me in his arms. *But in the dream,* I reminded myself, *Jesse and I end up together.*

I glanced over at my parents. My dad looked like he was yelling, and my mom's head was buried in her hands. I looked up at Jesse. His head was so close to mine, I could feel his breath on my cheek. His face was gentle, kind, trustworthy. My eyes traveled to Rachel, who was slow dancing with

Tommy. Her head was resting against his chest, and she looked blissfully happy. She caught my gaze and gave me the thumbs-up. "Go for it!" Rachel mouthed, motioning to Jesse.

And suddenly it occurred to me. I had a choice. I could be like my parents: I could stay bitter and angry and refuse to trust anybody. Or I could be like Jesse—and even Rachel. I could take a chance on love even though I knew it didn't always work out.

I thought that by resisting Jesse, I could avoid turning out like my parents. But I could see now the opposite was true. My parents had forgotten how to trust, but Jesse knew how all along, and he was trying to teach me.

I stopped dancing and pulled away from Jesse. "I don't want to be like them," I said suddenly.

"You're *not* like them," he insisted, knowing exactly who I meant, "and you don't have to be either."

As I gazed at Jesse, I felt sure that he was right. For the first time in a long while my jumble of emotions became clear. I knew exactly what I wanted.

The moon was high and full, and the night breeze was cool against my bare arms. I smelled the salty ocean air and felt the soft sand under my bare feet. I held my shoes in one hand and Jesse's hand in the other as I led him down the deserted beach to the edge of the ocean. The sounds of music and laughter from inside the club were muted by the rolling tide as I gazed up at the sky full of stars.

I let go of Jesse's hand and turned to face him. His

warm, tender eyes seemed to glow in the moonlight. For once I didn't try to hold my feelings back.

I pulled him close and kissed him. He met my lips with equal passion. I still heard the sound of the waves hitting the shore, but at that moment I felt like the rest of the world had disappeared.

By the time we came up for air, we were sitting together on the sand, not caring that our party clothes were rumpled and sandy. Resting in Jesse's arms, with the ocean breeze in my hair, my parents' divorce seemed as far away as my fears. The only thing that remained was the happy feeling I had from being with Jesse and the thought of spending the rest of the summer together. And I vowed right then that I would let nothing take that feeling away from me.

"I'm so happy," I murmured. "Let's never leave here."

Jesse kissed my forehead. "That sounds good to me," he said. "I could stay here forever."

"Look at the sky," I said. "There are so many stars."

"Hey," Jesse whispered. "There's the Big Dipper. Can you see it?"

I looked up to where he was pointing. I *could* see it, clearly. I saw the constellation so easily now, I couldn't believe that I'd had trouble making it out before.

"Yes," I told him, snuggling closer to him. "I see it. I see it perfectly."

*Do you ever wonder about falling in love? About members of the opposite sex? Do you need a little friendly advice but have no one to turn to? Well, that's where we come in . . . Jenny and Jake. Send us those questions you're dying to ask, and we'll give you the straight scoop on life and love in the nineties.*

## DEAR JAKE

**Q:** *I've got a huge problem. I think my best friend, Jon, likes me. He always hangs out at my house and wants to go for long walks in the evening. He constantly asks me if I like his girlfriend, if I think they're right for each other, and if I can think of a better match for him. His girlfriend and my boyfriend are starting to get suspicious. What should I do?*

*SC, Lexa, AR*

**A:** What you need to do is hint to Jon, ever so gently, that while you love having him as a friend, it will never go further than that. The next time you're sitting around with him watching movies or whatever, mention how cool it is having a good friend like him. Tell him he's like the brother you never had. If you have a brother, say it's like having a brother who doesn't steal your CDs or read your diary.

If Jon doesn't have a crush on you, he'll like the

compliment. If he does, it will let him know you're not romantically interested without any embarrassment on either side. Chances are he'll cool it with the Casanova act and things will go back to normal. If he continues to flirt, politely tell him to quit it. He knows you have a boyfriend. Only as a last resort should you have a Big Talk. One of those will just make you both uncomfortable.

**Q:** *I met this guy named Mike, and I think he's really cute. The problem is, he's always smoking pot with his friends. I've told him that I'm worried about him, but he always tells me it's no big deal. I really care about him, and I don't know what to do.*

*BJ, Rome, NY*

**A:** It's great that you're so concerned about your friend and that you realize smoking pot is a bad idea. It makes your brain muddled and confused, leaving you with about as much personality as boiled cabbage. And while not everyone who smokes pot goes on to harder drugs, almost all people with serious drug addictions began by smoking marijuana. In short, it's bad news.

So be there for Mike, but don't hang around him when he's smoking with his buddies—it will only make you uncomfortable and maybe even pressured to try it yourself. (For more information on what that would be like, see cabbage reference.) Tell him why smoking pot is anything but cool, but then back off. If you keep lecturing him, he'll eventually stop listening. If it gets to the point where his smoking is ruining your friendship, say sayonara and move on. Anyone who would choose drugs over a true friend is no one you need in your life.

Q: *I really like this guy, Colin, and he's told me he likes me too. The problem is, he made this really stupid contract with his best friend. He said he wouldn't ask me out until after we graduated high school or he would have to pay his friend twenty dollars. Can you believe that? I know his best friend doesn't like me, but isn't a contract to keep us from being together a little over the top? Colin is the only guy I like, and if I have to wait until after graduation to be with him I might explode!*

*SY, Burke, VA*

A: Talk about messed-up priorities! First of all, it's ridiculous that Colin would let twenty dollars stand in the way of an awesome relationship with you. And second, the fact that he even signed that "contract" in the first place is totally sick. His friend is insane to think he can claim power over who Colin dates. Colin is even more insane for agreeing.

You need to have a talk with this guy. If he likes you, why did he make this agreement? Now that he knows you like him, why doesn't he just fork over the cash? Better yet, why doesn't he just tell his friend to buzz off? These are questions you need to have answered. If he can't do this for you, if he can't blow off this immature game he's playing, then he's not worth another moment of your time.

## DEAR JENNY

**Q:** *Help! I'm totally in love with my boyfriend, Nick, but someone's trying to break us up. Nick and I go to different schools, and even though I have lots of guy friends, I would never cheat on him. But this girl, Tasha, keeps calling him and saying that I'm seeing two other guys! Now Nick isn't sure he can trust me anymore, and he's getting really distant. He's even stopped saying he loves me. This totally hurts. How can I convince him that he's the only guy I want?*

*TJ, Sanford, NC*

**A:** You need to have a talk with Nick, fast. Arrange to have a special night with him where you can really be alone and talk, perhaps in a quiet restaurant. Tell him that you understand how the rumors about you must confuse him, but that he really needs to listen to your side of the story. Try not to sound accusatory or angry. Assure him that you truly do love him, and remind him of the things you do to show it (that card you wrote him on his birthday, the way you always cheer him up when he's down, etc.).

Hopefully Nick will realize how much he means to you and that you would never do anything to jeopardize your relationship. Let him know how much it hurts that he can't seem to trust you. You should also point out that you trust him enough not to believe the silly rumors about him. Most likely he'll see that you're telling the truth, and with luck you can put your heads together and figure out why Tasha's trying to sabotage your relationship.

**Q:** *I'm in love with a friend of mine named Ryan. We get along well, and he's really sweet to me, but he's in love with another girl and only considers me his friend. What hurts me the most is that Ryan is in love with my best friend, Sara. Every time I catch him staring at her, I feel a stab of jealousy. What I don't understand is why he loves Sara so much when she doesn't care if he's alive. I really care for this guy, and my feelings seem to grow more every day. I just don't know what to do anymore. Please help!*

*MG, Philippines*

**A:** Loving someone who doesn't return your feelings is one of the most painful experiences anyone can go through. Hard as it may be, you really need to try to be a good friend to Ryan now.

He's going through the same thing with Sara. There may be a future for you and Ryan, but now is not the time. Be there to listen to him and offer advice, the way you know he would for you.

If Sara and Ryan do go out, try your best to support them, although you might not want to hang out with them when they're together. If Sara continues to ignore Ryan, eventually he'll stop obsessing. I know it may be tempting to tell him exactly how you feel, but this probably isn't a good idea for now. If he really only considers you a friend, it could make things uncomfortable. Try to meet other guys, but don't completely give up on Ryan. After all, most couples are friends first. Just be sure to wait until the time is right.

**Q:** *In the past few years I've gained a lot of weight. I feel like a slob, and I'm really unsure when it comes to stuff like guys. People say I have a beautiful face, but I feel like the ugliest person on earth. I'm trying to lose weight, but it's taking forever.*

*Last year I met a really nice guy named Ken. He's my math partner, and he's funny, smart, and sweet. On top of all that he's really cute. I want to be able to talk to him, but every time I get up my courage, I eventually back down. I keep thinking he would never want to date someone who looks like me. What should I do?*

*KC, Omaha, NE*

**A:** You're not alone. Almost every girl your age

is self-conscious about her body. Who can blame you? With the media shoving stick-thin models in our faces all time, it's easy to feel that our own bodies don't measure up.

But if you worry too much about what you look like, you're going to miss out on a lot of fun and a lot of great guys. Look at the way you described Ken. You wrote that he was funny, smart, and sweet. The fact that he was cute was the last thing you mentioned. Obviously his terrific personality is more important to you than what he looks like. People can gain weight, lose weight, dye their hair, or totally change their style, but what's most attractive about any person is what they are like inside.

Stop worrying about that extra weight and start concentrating on what makes you a special, wonderful person. You can even make a list of your best qualities: your sense of humor, your talents, the great advice you give. This will help you remember why you're someone worth knowing. If you take a look around at the most popular kids at your school, you'll notice a trend. Most of them probably don't have flawless faces and bodies, but they do have confidence. Confidence is a key factor in success and happiness, but no one can give it to you. You have to build it yourself. You have a choice: You can spend the rest of your life upset about what you could be or should be——or you can revel in all the fantastic things that you are.

If you're really set on losing weight, however, do it sensibly. The key is to have fun. Take up in-line skating or swimming so you can burn calories while having a great time. And definitely go for Ken. He seems like a great guy. Make an effort to talk to him at school. It can be about anything: how lame your teacher is, what new movies are out, or how his weekend was. And while you're talking about movies, you might want to casually ask if he'd like to see one with you sometime. The worst that can happen is he'll say no. If he does, you can deal. Confident people aren't afraid to take risks. And here's a trick: If you don't feel confident at any given moment, fake it. No one will know the difference, and you may even fool yourself.

*Do you have questions about love? Write to:*

Jenny Burgess or Jake Korman
c/o Daniel Weiss Associates
33 West 17th Street
New York, NY 10011

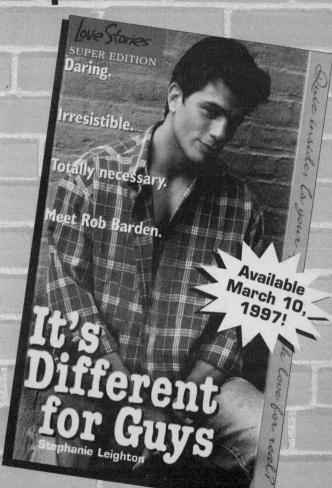